# PATCH

# **P**ATCH

by

Catherine Robinson

HAMILTON & Co. Publishers
**LONDON**

**Paperback ISBN 1 901668 70 3**

**Publisher**

HAMILTON & Co. Publishers
10 Stratton Street
Mayfair
**London**

# CHAPTER ONE

"Joe! Will you stop kicking that ball!" That was Joe's mum. Boom-skitter. Boom-skitter. That was the ball.

"Joe!"

Joe gave the ball one last hard slam against the kitchen wall, gruffly folded his arms and threw himself onto the sofa in a sulk. His mum turned to him, still drying her hands on the tea cloth.

"What is wrong with you?"

"I'm bored."

"Well call for Ashley and Bradley."

"They've gone to pony club." His mum sighed. That again.

"Joe," she said, (she was using that voice she used when she'd already explained something to him half a dozen times), "when we find a suitable pony for you, we'll buy it."

"What was wrong with the one we saw yesterday?"

"It was fifteen hundred pounds, that's what."

Joe sighed. He knew he was behaving like a spoilt brat, but almost since Fudge had died three months ago, he'd been longing to ride again. At first he was too upset to think about another pony, Fudge had been such a kind old man, but now Ashley and Bradley were riding their ponies every night and going to pony club nearly every weekend, and Joe couldn't join in. It wasn't fair. He stood and stomped upstairs.

"I'm going to play on my computer!"

"The trouble with you is you don't know when you're well off my lad!" shouted his mother. "When I was your age I'd have given anything for a pony, and computers weren't even thought of!" Not that old chestnut again. Joe knew these lines so well he was able to mouth them with her as he climbed the stairs.

He didn't really want to play on his computer, he wanted to go and play with Ashley and Bradley or go to pony club, or both. He didn't really want to be horrible to his mum either. It just worked out that way. In the end being horrible to his mum only made him feel more rotten. He threw himself on his bed and picked up last week's copy of ***"Horse and Hound."*** He flicked to the classifieds to see what other people were riding, and there it was, staring up at him under ***Horses for Sale***

***"12 hh grey gelding. A real character £650."***

He bounced up, suddenly alive, and dashed downstairs.

"Mum! Mum!" he screeched. "Look!" He thrust the advertisement under her nose. "See! It's even a fairly local phone number."

"I know love," his mum said, (this time she was using her speak-to-him-gently-or-he-might-explode voice). "I saw the advert but I didn't like that ***"a real character"***, it probably means it's naughty."

"Oh but mum p-l-e-a-s-e."

His mum sighed, the pony had probably gone anyway, the magazine was more than a week old. Besides, a phone call didn't mean they had to buy it, and it would shut Joe up. Defeated she took the magazine from him and picked up the receiver. Joe punched the air in triumph and gave a cry of "Yes!"

He didn't hear the content of the phone call. He was too busy jumping on the sofa in the living room and whispering "yes! yes! yes!" to himself. The pony was going to be the right one. He could tell. He knew. Sure enough, the pony hadn't been sold, which further convinced his mother that there was something wrong with it, but nonetheless she'd agreed to try it that afternoon.

"Go on then! Move yourself!" she shouted "Jodhs on! We're to be there in an hour."

Joe dashed upstairs, two steps at a time and squirmed into his jodhpurs. He was still fastening them at the bottom of the stairs when his mother handed him his hat.

During the half-hour journey to Oak Tree Stables, she treated Joe to a half-hour monologue as to why they wouldn't buy the pony. The gist of it was that, she never liked buying from dealers as she didn't trust them, at that price the pony would already have been sold if it was any good and Joe's father wasn't there today. Joe thought that the last reason was irrelevant. Although his father was a rider, he never gave Joe's ponies a second glance.

Oak Tree Stables, when they saw it, was a sorry dump. Joe's mother managed to raise her eyebrows and purse her lips at the same time. This saved her the effort of having to say, "this is exactly what I thought it would be like." The ramshackle stables were set in bare paddocks where the only green was provided by long stalks of poisonous ragwort. Joe ignored her. His eyes were on the fat little grey pony, which was being led from the stable in front of him. The pony looked straight at Joe and sardonically closed one eye.

"He winked at me mum! He winked at me!"

"Yes Joe."

"He did mum, honest!" Joe winked back.

Joe's mum looked the pony up and down. She walked around it. She ran her hands down its legs. She stood back and then looked the groom in the eyes.

"What's that scar on its hock?"

"Old injury," he answered.

"Can we see it tacked up?" she asked. Joe breathed a sigh of relief. It had passed the first test. They'd walked away from some ponies before they'd seen them ridden.

A fat girl brought out a saddle that was too big, and plonked it on the pony's back. Despite the fact that she weighed at least ten stone the girl sat on the pony and put it through its paces. It even jumped a small course of fences with her. Joe's mum was looking more interested. "Do you want a go now?" she asked. Joe nodded and put on his hat. Even as he mounted the pony, it felt right. It stood quietly as he swung his leg into place and moved away at his first command. The pony trotted obediently, cantered smoothly and jumped boldly. Joe was grinning from ear to ear as he walked the pony back to his mum. She still didn't smile. "Let's see it in traffic," she said.

Joe dismounted and the groom led the pony out onto the busy main road where it strode on as motorbikes, buses, and juggernauts thundered past.

"See!" Joe shouted "there's nothing wrong with him!" Joe's mum still hadn't smiled. She gestured to him with a crooked finger. "Joe," she explained "it's not very pretty." She was looking at the hairless pink rings around its knowing brown eyes.

"I don't care!" Joe answered.

His mother sighed. In all truth, she could find nothing else wrong with the pony. She was assured that it had no vices, it had done everything right in a saddle that didn't fit, and Joe clearly loved it already - but she felt strangely uneasy. If it was so reliable why hadn't it already been sold? When she asked the groom that question, he merely shrugged in answer. She sighed again. If the pony really was this, good he was a bargain, ugly or not.

"Will you take £500?" she asked, half hoping her offer would be refused. When the groom nodded, she didn't feel entirely pleased. Joe did! He was hissing "yes! Yes! Yes!" and punching the air again.

"I'll call him Patch," Joe announced, "because of the pink patches round his eyes." Joe's mum fumbled with the car keys; "I don't know what your dad'll say."

# CHAPTER TWO

"Pig," Joe's dad said.

"What?"

"You should have called it Pig, not Patch, it's as fat as one."

"We can put it on a diet," Joe said. Patch swung his head from side to side over the stable door.

"I hope it doesn't weave. That's all we flaming need."

"That's not weaving!" Joe answered. "He's just telling us he doesn't want to go on a diet, aren't you Patch?" and he kissed the pony's nose.

As his lips made contact Patch suddenly snorted and blasted out pony snot. Joe wiped his face, squealed "yuk", and "gross". His father laughed. "Well, at least its got a sense of humour - and it'll need one looking like that."

His mum had insisted they let Patch settle in, meet the other horses and get used to the place before Joe could ride him, so Joe passed the week by bringing a stream of visitors to the stable yard to meet Patch, and the less they knew about horses, the more they liked him.

Joe's grandma knew nothing about horses. She'd spent thirty eight years married to a show jumper and had made certain that she never so much as picked up a dandy brush. To her, horses were expensive beasts that meant muck got trodden into the carpet. She'd only become more tolerant of them now that the muck was being trodden into Carol's carpet. Joe dragged her into the stable.

"What do you think grandma?"

"Ooo! He's lovely! Aren't you lucky, eh? What a lucky lad. I'll bet all your friends at school wish he was their's, don't they?" Joe grinned at the pony who stood munching his hay. "I like his eyes," his grandma went on, "I've never seen a pony with eyes like that. Isn't it unusual? What does your dad think?"

"My dad thinks he's too fat."

"You can't suit some folk can you? Well, me and you like him, don't we love?" and she patted Patch gently on his neck.

Bradley was always diplomatic, so he said nothing, but Ashley laughed. "That Joe, is ***well*** ugly," he said.

"You'll be laughing on the other side of your face when we start winning stuff," Joe answered, and he winked at Patch. Patch winked back. Bradley nodded wisely.

"It doesn't matter what they look like, it's what they do." Patch threw his head up and down in agreement.

"That's so fat it can hardly walk," sneered Ashley. Joe didn't mind. Patch wouldn't always be fat, and he liked the pink rings round his eyes.

Patch seemed to settle in quickly. Within days the big white tomcat had moved in with him and was sleeping in his stable. The German Shepherd dog put two front feet on the stable door and stood nose to nose with him, and Gyp, the Border Collie, left Patch alone. (That in itself was almost a miracle as Gyp nipped the heels of anything with four legs and most things with two). In the field, Patch was quiet. He grazed or he stood nose to nose with Joe's dad's big mare and her foal. Joe liked to watch Patch. He laughed at the way Patch seemed to know what was going on. If Joe offered him a mint, he threw his head up and down. If the foal plunged and bucked around the field Patch curled his lip as if he were laughing. Joe could see why the advert for him had said "a real character".

By Saturday Joe's mum was satisfied that Patch had settled in and agreed that Joe could ride him. Joe was excited all morning. He tacked Patch up in his brand new saddle and bridle.

Joe mounted up and, smiling confidently, he walked quietly to the arena. He rode a few circuits, feeling glad to be back in the saddle, and then kicked for a trot. Patch ignored him. Joe kicked again, harder. Patch ignored him.

"Do you want a stick?" Joe's mum called from her place by the fence. Joe nodded sternly and kicked again.

"Come on Patch," he growled. This time Patch trotted.

"He's lazy!' his mum called. "We'll have to start that diet."

Joe pointed Patch at a small cross pole and kicked on. Patch trotted at it keenly - but at the last second he planted his two front feet! Without speaking Joe took the stick from his mum and trotted on again. He didn't like to smack a pony but he knew that a pony can't be allowed to think he's the boss, or he can be dangerous. Besides, Patch was probably testing him out, seeing how much he could get away with. Joe rode for the fence again, "you can do this," he was saying in his head. Patch pricked his ears, picked up his pace and headed for it - then stopped abruptly right in front of it! Quickly Joe raised his stick and whacked the pony's flank. In the same second Patch flicked up his back feet and dumped Joe in the sand. Breathless and shocked Joe looked up. Patch hadn't moved but was curling a top lip as he looked down at him. Joe's mum was running across the arena. Her heart had sunk as far as her wellies. This was exactly the sort of thing she'd been afraid of. Why had the pony waited until she'd paid five hundred quid for it before it misbehaved? Joe was on his feet again and scrambling back into the saddle.

"He laughed at me mum! I saw him laugh at me!"

She looked sternly at Patch. The pony met her gaze and slowly closed, then opened one eye before walking off.

She waited for a moment then she spoke.

"Don't try to jump him again Joe," she said at last, "just walk him on a loose rein. It could be that saddle. We'll get it checked."

That evening she couldn't concentrate. She was trying to watch ***Brookside*** but she couldn't forget that pony's face. She made a cup of tea then plumped up the cushions. She picked up a magazine, then put it down, and then plumped up the cushions again.

"What's the matter with you?" her husband asked, fed up of it. "That pony," she said finally, "it winked at me Robert."

"Carol! You sound like Joe."

"I know it sounds daft, but I saw it. It laughed at Joe when he was on the floor, and when he got back on it, it winked at me."

"Carol, ponies don't wink and they don't laugh."

"That's why I told him not to try it again, it as good as told me it would throw him off again." Robert folded his newspaper.

"It's trying it on! It wants a good hiding. That’s all. You've been listening to Joe's daft talk."

Robert had been brought up in farming and there had been horses around him all his life. His father had show jumped and he'd met every sort of horse or pony at one time or another - but never one that winked. He knew his horses, he liked his horses, but he stood no nonsense. They did things Robert's way or not at all.

"Look," he said "get some fat off it and get that saddle checked. At five hundred quid we can't lose. If it’s no better by the Autumn, it goes - okay?" Carol nodded but she wasn't happy.

"You know," she confided "I never really liked that pony from the moment I saw it. I can't tell you why."

"Trust your instincts. That’s what my old dad used to say, trust your instincts."

A lot of use that advice was now. Joe bounced in.

"Have the horses had their hay?" His mum shook her head.

"I'll go and do it."

"Joe," she called after him, "one lap for Patch, no more."

# CHAPTER THREE

Steady drizzle was blowing across the yard. In the light of the halogen lamp Joe could see it billowing in waves. He turned up his coat collar to walk the few steps from the farmhouse door to the barn. He called the dogs to him from the wash room.

Joe liked to give the horses their night time hay, but only if the dogs were with him. He'd never admit to being frightened of the dark - well, it wasn't the dark so much as the silence and the shadows he didn't like, but the dogs explored the shadows and broke the silence as they padded about with their claws clicking on the concrete.

He took two bulging haynets to Regan and her foal, and then stood, watching them. He put his arms up to hold Regan's strong brown neck and buried his nose in her silky horsy smell as she chomped with a steady rhythm on her hay. Little Taz, her colt foal, seemed to tip toe up to him. Joe squatted on his haunches so as not to tower over him. Taz nibbled at Joe's collar and pulled his anorak toggle with his teeth. Joe stayed still and watchful, enjoying the moment, watching his breath and the foal's breath mingle in silent clouds. He squatted there quietly until his legs ached, then gently stood and made his way back to the barn. He picked up one lap of hay, put it in a net and crossed the yard to

Patch. He tied the haynet to the ring in a slip-knot, patted Patch and was unbolting the stable door when he heard a voice behind him.

"Is that all I get then?"

"Yes it is, you fat pig..."

Joe swung round. Patch had spoken! He stood for a minute and stared, his heart beating so loudly he could hear it, his eyes held open so wide they felt cold. The white cat had raised his head and he too was watching with ears pricked, from the corner. Joe had replied before he'd realised! The silence hung in the damp air for what seemed like ages. "Did you speak to me?" Joe asked.

Patch winked. "You did, didn't you?" Patch turned away.

"I know you did Patch, I heard you, it's no good pretending you didn't." Patch chomped on his hay. Joe waited for an answer.

Nothing.

Perhaps it was just his imagination after all? Why had the cat looked up then?

"You can talk, can't you?"

Patch ignored him, still chomping. Joe walked round to his head.

"Say something else and you can have some more hay."

"You're on," Patch answered. Joe let out a squawk - a mixture of triumph and shock!

"You can talk! You can damn, flaming, blasted talk!"

"Okay, okay calm down kid. I forgot myself when I saw how skinny you were being with that hay. I don't normally talk to people. Now get this hay, eh?"

"I'll get it! I'll get it!"

Joe dashed across the stable yard babbling to the dogs, "D'you hear that? Yogi? Gyp? Patch can talk! Wait till I tell my mum!" He scooped up an armful of hay and flung it over the stable door, dancing from foot to foot and shrieking and laughing as he did so. "I never knew you could talk!"

"There's a lot you don't know about me," Patch answered with his mouth full, "but no telling."

"No," said Joe, "just my mum and dad." Patch walked to the stable door. "Especially not your mum and dad. Look kid, if word got out I'd be on TV, in the circus, you name it, I'd be there. They'd sell me, I'm worth a mint."

"Oh," Joe was disappointed "I'd not thought of that."

"No, I've watched you, there's quite a lot you don't think about. I, on the other hand, think and as you now know I can talk, I might as well make the most of it. I'd like a written contract. Terms and Conditions of Employment, that sort of thing."

"You want what?" Joe asked.

"I heard about it when I was at Oak Tree Stables. The grooms had one. So, bring a pen and paper." Joe nodded, "I'll do it in the morning. If I don't hurry up now my mum will come looking for me." Joe hesitated for a moment, "Can you write as well?" The pony let out a huge guffaw.

"Don't be ridiculous!" he laughed, "I'm a pony, ***you'll*** have to write it." "Okay Patch - goodnight" and Joe turned to walk away.

"And another thing, my name is not Patch, never has been."

"Oh? What is it?"

"They call me..." Patch hesitated, "well, that doesn't matter. You can call me, Sir."

"All right, good night - Sir" Joe said and he whistled for the dogs and set off back to the house.

# CHAPTER FOUR

He wasn't sure about this at all, calling a pony "sir". What would his dad say? You call the boss "sir", and Joe was supposed to be the boss, not Patch. And what was all this about a written contract? He didn't like it at all. The pony made him feel stupid. It knew words he didn't know. It said he didn't think, and it wanted to be called sir. Joe sighed as he prised his wellie off.

"You were a long time love," his mum remarked.

"I was talking to Patch," Joe answered, "is there a dictionary in here?"

"Why?" Joe's dad asked, "Patch use big words, did he?"

Joe shot his dad a quick glance but he was too busy laughing at his own joke to notice.

Joe flicked through the dictionary, ***contraband, contraception, contract!..*** He read: ***"contract mutual especially business agreement; agreement enforceable by law."***

Therefore, Patch wanted to strike a deal, make a bargain. He'd have to think about this.

That night Joe barely slept. He lay awake for hours, on his back, on his front, on his side. No matter how hard he tried, sleep just wouldn't come. He counted sheep, counted ponies, and emptied his mind. When sleep did come it was disturbed by the din of arguing animals all demanding to be called your grace or m' lord". There were ducks holding out dishes and teacups for him to fill from a silver jug. The dogs put a collar and lead on him, the white tom cat chased him round the yard with a whip whilst Patch, smoking a cigarette in his stable, laughed and laughed.

Joe woke again a five thirty, sweating now and feeling as exhausted as when he first went to bed. When he opened his eyes, his first consolation was that it had probably all been a dream. He needed to be certain. He climbed out of bed, pulled on his Blackburn Rovers track suit over his pyjamas, headed for the door and called the dogs.

He walked out onto the yard and peeped over Patch's door. Patch raised his head from the straw.

"What time do you call this kid!" Joe sighed deeply. It was true. "Half past five sir."

"Half past five! I've not been up at this time since I was pulling a milk float! Have you brought that pen and paper?"

"I'll get them," said Joe, "whilst there's no one about."

Joe returned with his pen and note pad and settled himself down in the straw. Patch cleared his throat.

“Right” he began, ***"Terms and conditions of employment for the 12 hh grey gelding ridden by Joe:***

***One: No jumping"***

"Oh! sir!" Joe exclaimed, slamming down his pencil, "That’s not fair!"

"Jumping is for mugs."

"You're a good jumper! You jumped brilliantly at Oak Tree Stables."

"Yep, and it worked a treat, you took me home..."

"But Patch..."

*"Two: No delivering milk."* Joe picked up his pencil, he knew there was no point in arguing.

***"Three: No sissy ribbons to be put in my tail or coloured brow bands on my bridle, or tinsel on any part of my body at Christmas."*** Joe wrote quickly to keep up. Patch was enjoying himself.

***"Four: No medicine will be accepted at any time."***

***"Five: No stick to be used."***

***"Six: At least five laps of hay each night."***

***"Seven: To be allowed to play out every day except in the worst of the weather and in return, I, the said grey gelding will allow Joe to ride me for one hour each week."***

With that, Patch leaned over and slobbered on the notepad by way of a signature.

Joe didn't speak. He stood up silently and walked out of the stable. "Hey kid! What about some hay?" Joe looked the pony in the face, "No chance," he said and walked across the yard.

The sun was up by now but his mum and dad weren't. Joe decided to walk the dogs round the fields and give the matter of this contract some thought. He whistled and Yogi and Gyp bounded to him, eager for an early walk. Joe took the note pad out of his pocket.

***"One: No jumping."*** That was ridiculous. They'd ***bought*** the pony to jump. He wasn't putting up with that. He wasn't a milkman, so number two wasn't a problem, and three he could tolerate, but his mum might need some persuading to go easy on the ribbons, especially at Christmas. (She'd got Fudge up like a Christmas tree last year, he'd even had baubles in his mane, but he could work on her.) What about four? ***No Medicine.*** The stupid pony! It needed to be wormed this week. He would die without medicine.

***Five: No stick.*** Joe felt like knocking it senseless at the moment. ***Six: Five laps of hay***. No way! Not only would that cost a fortune, his mother wouldn't put up with it and it was bad for the pony. He got to play out every day as it was, so seven was okay. That last bit though, ***"will allow Joe to ride me for one hour each week."***

What a cheek!

Joe sat on the stile and counted on his fingers. He did twenty-five hours a week in school, an hour a day on the stables, not counting homework and making his bed and emptying the washing machine. That made at least thirty eight hours work a week, and that fat idle blob wanted to do an hour! One hour! "No way." Joe said aloud, "no way".

Still, Joe realised that Patch was a pretty tough character. He'd obviously been around a bit. Joe would have to be crafty with this or he'd end up on the floor again. Of course, *he* hadn't signed that contract yet, so it hadn't been agreed. He'd have to draw up a contract of his own then try to meet Patch half way.

"Joe! Joe!" That was his dad's voice. "Joe! The blasted dog!" Joe saw that Gyp was in the bottom paddock, running the ewes legless.

"Gyp! Gyp! Come here!" he screeched at him too late. As he did so he could hear fragments of his father's ranting in the distance, "Can't control it, shouldn't be walking it in the first place - more sense - lost a lamb - you'll pay for it - this time of the morning..." By now Joe had a panting Gyp by the collar and the ewes were breathless and bulgey eyed in the bottom corner of the field. His dad approached, grabbed the dog from him, gave him a swift clout round the ear and followed it with one for the dog.

"That's for worrying me and your mother sick!"

"There's no need to hit the dog," Joe said.

"No. You're right. That was your fault as well. I should have given you another! Now get up that field before I do!"

Joe burst into tears and set off at a furious march, sniffing and squealing. Yogi loped after him, grinning all over his doggy face.

"Shut up," Joe shouted at him "just 'cos you weren't thumped!"

Joe wasn't angry at the dog, or even bothered about being thumped, but ever since that pony had opened its mouth, everything had gone wrong. He'd hardly slept, he'd had bad dreams, he'd let the dog chase the sheep, he'd got in trouble with his dad and his pony had been totally unreasonable. He wished it had kept its mouth shut.

As the wash room door clicked open, his mother came flapping to him in her backless slippers and pink dressing gown.

"Oh! thank God! What got into you? Where have you been? Are you alright? Where's Gyp? Why are you crying?" (She did that sometimes, his mum. Asked a load of questions but didn't leave any room for you to answer them.)

'I took the dogs for a walk. Gyp chased the sheep, so my dad's seeing to them." Joe walked away and made for the stairs. "I'm going back to bed."

"What about your breakfast?"

"I don't want any."

# CHAPTER FIVE

The sheep were sweated and startled. Robert's horses were his pleasure but his sheep were his livelihood. Fortunately they had two-month-old lambs at foot and Gyp had enjoyed the chase but he wasn't a worrier. Robert settled the flock, pushed Gyp into the wash room and turned the horses out. Regan and Taz first, and then Patch. He put on Patch's headcollar, then turned and looked at him critically. The last thing that pony needed was to stuff its face on spring grass for seven hours. He turned it round, led it back into the stable and bolted the door.

"I've left Patch in," he told his wife as he washed his hands at the sink a few minutes later.

"That should get some fat of it. Give Joe a shout, he'll have to ride it."

"He's asleep," Carol explained. Robert stopped.

"Asleep? What's the matter with that child?" He shook his head. His ten year old son was a mystery to him that deepened daily.

When Joe opened his eyes at last it was to see the daylight beginning to fade in the evening sky. He looked at his bedside clock, eight thirty. He'd slept all day. He stood up. He was sweaty, he was still wearing his pyjamas under his tracksuit. It was hardly worth taking them off now. He felt hungry. He walked downstairs' and into the living room.

"Oh, its up then," his father remarked without taking his eyes from the sports Section of the Sunday Times. Joe's mum looked up, she had the colour supplement open on her knee.

"Are you not well love?"

"I just didn't sleep well last night."

"No," his father put in, still not looking up, "you won't sleep tonight now either, will you? Or do you plan to stay up all night? Is this your latest fad, after recycling aluminium cans and transcendental meditation?"

"Leave him alone Robert!" Joe's mother snapped. "He's not well."

"I'm all right," Joe answered.

"Well if you're all right you should have been up," his dad went on, "not skulking in bed all day after a well deserved wallop. That pony of yours has stood in all day waiting for you to ride it."

A shaft of horror shot through Joe. They'd kept Patch in, after he'd said in his contract that he wanted to play out every day. What would this mean? What would he do now? He tried not to let his panic show on his face. His throat felt tight and dry but he needed to speak.

"How much hay did you give him?" he asked

"None," his father answered, "that's the point of keeping him in. He's had a lap just now. He's staying in tomorrow as well so you'll have to ride him after school."

Not on your Nellie, thought Joe. Not in a million years, but he smiled and nodded. His mum offered him a beef sandwich but he'd suddenly lost his appetite again. She came over and felt his forehead. He must be sickening for something. Joe sloped back upstairs.

Great. His dad had just broken two parts of the contract in one day, planned to do the same tomorrow and then expected Joe to ride! What could he do? He sat with his head in his hands.

He could keep up this sickness thing for a few more days. He'd already got his mother convinced and it would buy him some time. It wasn't a long term solution though. He could go out there and apologise to Patch, explain that it had been out of his hands, that he'd been asleep all day. He didn't want to do that though. He'd grovelled enough to that pony already. He wanted to find a way of striking a better deal, not give Patch a reason to think he was agreeing to this one.

That was it. He'd have to draw up his own contract. He wasn't tired so he'd stay up tonight and draw up a new contract, then he'd convince his mum he was too ill for school tomorrow, and discuss it with Patch. He'd have to wait until his dad went out though. He usually went to the auction on Monday, so there was a good chance of getting away with it. He rummaged in his tracksuit pocket and pulled out the slobbered on contract. He tore the top sheet from the note pad and lay it on his desk. He sat down, picked up his pencil and began afresh.

***Terms and Conditions of Employment for the 12 hands gelding, ridden by Joe,*** then he stopped. He would list first, all the terms he could agree to easily, so that Patch might think he was getting his own way. He continued to write:

***One. No delivering milk.***

***Two. No sissy ribbons to be put in Patch's tail or coloured browbands on his bridle, or tinsel on any part of his body at Christmas.***

***Three. No unnecessary medicine to be given .*** (He was proud of that one, "unnecessary". It was a big word. He'd had it in a spelling test last week and got it right. It half sounded like he was agreeing with Patch. From now on it would be tricky though.)

***Four. Patch to be allowed to play out at grass every day, except a) in the worst weather and b) when he's too fat .*** (Joe hesitated, Patch wouldn't like that one)

***Five. One lap of hay to be given until such time as Patch has lost weight then he can have more.*** (He wouldn't like that either.)

He looked back at Patch's contract, what hadn't he covered? ***"No stick to be used."*** If he bucks me off, I'll batter him, Joe thought. Then it came to him, he smiled as he wrote, ***Six. No stick to be used by Joe and no bucking off to be used by Patch. Patch will allow Joe to ride him for up to eight hours a week, and that includes up to two hours of jumping.*** Joe signed it with a flourish and drew a smiling face in the curve of his ***"J".*** He sat back and read it over. Even if Patch agreed to all this, which he knew was highly unlikely, he still didn't feel happy. Why should he have to call him "sir"?

He squeezed in a seventh item

***Seven. Joe has no need to address Patch as sir.***

Joe sat back and read it again. Did it really matter what he called him so long as Patch would jump and lose weight? Was he just being petty? There was no point in asking for trouble. Then he thought of it! He crossed out seven and started again.

***"Seven. Joe to address Patch as "sir", provided Patch will address Joe as "sir".*** That was fair enough.

His page was a mess now so he ripped it out and he wrote it all out again, neatly. He looked at his clock. It was nearly ten o'clock but he wasn't tired so he played on his computer for a while. His mum came up with tea and toast and felt his forehead again. She walked away, muttering about growing pains or something.

Even whilst zapping Robotnik with a spinning Sonic the Hedgehog Joe was considering the problem of his talking pony. He never would have thought it could be so difficult. It wouldn't be so bad, thought Joe, if the pony was a nice person. Regan or Taz wouldn't be so bossy or stubborn or superior. "Sir" indeed! Who does he think he is? He couldn't help smiling though, at the thought of his friend's faces if only they knew! He'd love to bring Ashley or Bradley on the yard and let them see Patch talk! He laughed at the thought of it. They'd be jealous, really jealous, and Patch would have something to say to Ashley for calling him ugly. Joe amused himself by making up scenes in his head, like a film, of Patch meeting his various friends. The only person Patch would be nice to was his Grandma. He wandered over to the window and watched the night sky for a while. What if Patch wouldn't meet him half way with this contract though? What then? Joe sighed deeply. What then? He heard the creak of the stairs as his mum and dad came up to bed. His mum put her head round his bedroom door.

"Don't stay up too late love and we'll see how you feel in the morning, eh?" Joe blew her a kiss and turned back to the window.

Then it hit him! Why then, it is impossible to say, but sometimes it happens like that. (Joe's dad was once frying an egg and he suddenly said, "I should have gone to the dentists on Friday." Perhaps it happens to everyone, that an idea dawns from nowhere, but it happened to Joe as he looked at the stars.) "If he doesn't agree to my contract, I'll phone the newspapers and I'll tell everyone he can talk, and I'll buy a decent pony with the money I raise!"

Joe suddenly felt as if a huge weight had been lifted from his shoulders. He felt the way you feel when you've finished a test, when you break up from school or when you wake up and remember it's your birthday. He crept under the duvet and slept a peaceful sleep.

As he lay awake, watching the strip of daylight cast on his dinosaur wallpaper through the gap in his curtains, a grin of contentment passed across Joe's face. He was quite looking forward to speaking to Patch again, now he knew he had some power. He'd only had ten minutes conversation with that pony, but worrying about what it said had taken up the best part of two days. He was wide awake. From his position in bed he reached out and pulled the curtain back, all he could see was blue stretching to the four corners of the window frame. His instinct was to bounce out of bed and get dressed but if he did that he'd be queuing up in the playground at five to nine. No. Better play it cooler.

His bedroom door clicked open.

"How're you feeling love?"

"A bit better than yesterday," Joe answered from under the duvet. (It was only a white lie. He did feel better than yesterday, except he felt a lot better!)

"Do you fancy a bit of breakfast?"

"Well, it might make me feel a bit better." He was ravenous. He fancied a fry up with two eggs, two sausages, bacon, fried bread and tomatoes all covered in brown sauce. "I'll just have a slice of dry toast," he moaned, weakly.

"Aren't you going to school?"

"I'll see how I feel after I've had the toast." - Best not to sound too enthusiastic about staying off school.

Joe sat on his bed and opened his curtains a crack. His dad was already on the yard, hefting a bale into the trailer. Good. That meant he must be taking those two old ewes to the auction. He watched his dad go about his morning jobs, it passed the time. He couldn't see the stables from his window but he could hear Patch neighing and kicking his door. Regan and Taz must be playing in the field again thought Joe, so Patch will be furious. He couldn't stop a sly smile from creeping across his features. His mum returned with the dry toast and a glass of milk. Why had he asked for it dry? He didn't like dry toast.

"On second thoughts," his mum said, "you'd be better off with water, it'll sit easier on your stomach," and she walked off with the milk. Great. He'd put up with enough because of this pony - just wait till he saw it!

# CHAPTER SIX

He saw it, as it turned out, at about eleven o'clock that morning. His dad had gone to the auction and although his mum had phoned the book shop to say she couldn't go to work, she'd agreed that a breath of fresh air might do Joe good. Gyp always went to the auction with Robert, so Joe whistled to Yogi who was lying, head on paws, sorry for himself, as he always did on auction days.

Joe strolled out, German Shepherd at his side, and when he reached Patch's door, he folded his arms and casually leaned on it.

"Hi ya Patch," he said.

Patch was looking vaguely through the mesh-covered window at the back of his stable. He didn't move.

"...sir" Joe added. Patch turned his head slowly, looked at Joe then turned back again.

"Fancy going out later?" Joe asked chirpily. Patch didn't respond. Joe went on, "when I say out of course, I mean ***ridden*** out, not playing out." Patch still didn't speak. "I'm on my own," Joe added, "you can answer." Patch gave a deep sigh. "I get it," Joe grinned, "you aren't speaking to me!" He let out squeal of laughter. "Great, I like it that way. Fudge never said a word and we got on like a house on fire. Cool."

Still no response from Patch.

"Well," said Joe "as you aren't in the mood for arguing, now is probably a good time to read you *my* Terms and Conditions of Your Employment." Patch turned from the window and pricked his ears forward. "It's no use looking like that," Joe protested, "I never agreed to your terms. These are mine."

Joe took the neatly folded note paper from the back pocket of his jeans and began to read.

***"One: no delivering milk***

He'd got as far as ***Four:...except when he's too fat*** before he got any response from Patch. Patch snorted loudly. At ***Five: one lap of hay to be given,*** Patch was snorting and curling his lip both at once, and by the time Joe had got to ***eight hours, including two hours of jumping,*** Patch was snorting, curling his lips and stamping the ground. (If he had been human, he would have been shrieking, holding his sides and rolling about with laughter.)

Twenty-four hours ago, this display of contempt for his ideas would have upset Joe but not now.

"You think it's funny do you?" Joe asked with a grin.

Patch raised his tail and dumped a huge mound of droppings in the straw before turning back to the window.

"Tell you what," Joe said, "next time you decide to learn something from humans, make it something useful, like how to use a toilet." He ambled across the yard, returned with the skip and the fork and began lifting Patch's mess out of the straw.

"So," he chatted, "at about tea time, I'll be out here with the saddle and we'll do the second of my eight hours, okay? You don't have to sign the contract of course, or even slobber on it, but, let's put it this way, I can think of at least two television programmes that would be really interested in a talking pony. I don't remember having seen one on ***Country file,*** or ***The Really Wild Show.***

What I really wanted all along you see, was a decent jumping pony, so if you aren't one, I'm not really bothered Patch. You've been nothing but a pain in the bum since you opened your mouth on Saturday night. I'll just sell you and buy one that jumps but doesn't talk. Think about it." Joe's heart was beating in his throat and he could feel his ears burning but he grinned at Patch smugly for a moment, then turned to unbolt the door.

Suddenly a gripping pain seized him right across his middle! He couldn't breathe. He dropped the fork he was carrying and grabbed frantically at his stomach. He coughed and wheezed. Patch was pulling the end of his belt with his teeth! Joe gasped.

“Let go. Let go you sod!...sir..." Patch let go then spoke for the first time that morning.

"Tighten my girth like that, ever, and you're off kid."

Joe straightened his belt, rose to his full height picked up the fork and walked out, trying to breathe normally

When he rounded the corner, he whacked Yogi on the head.

"Where were you? Useless! Where were you when my pony was trying to kill me?"

If you've ever tried to smack a German Shepherd on the head you'll know their skulls are very hard. Joe just found this out. He held his own hand and sucked in air sharply between his teeth. Yogi grinned his daft doggy grin.

By the time Joe left the house wearing his riding hat, five hours later, he'd managed to convince himself that it was all going to be okay. Even though Patch had nearly squeezed his breath out, he hadn't argued about the contract.

Joe picked up his grooming kit saddle and bridle from the wash room. Gyp wasn't back so Yogi was still looking miserable. Joe went out, led Patch onto the yard, tied him up and brushed him. "Blackmail they call this," Patch muttered.

"Do they? Well bullying is what they call what you were doing to me." Patch didn't speak again and Joe just said things like "come on then" and "move over" - the things you'd say to an ordinary pony. Joe saddled up, gently tightened the girth and lead Patch into the arena. Patch behaved like a good, well schooled pony. He trotted, head down, moved from Joe's leg when he was asked, cantered evenly, and stopped squarely as soon as Joe sat into him.

"Look," Joe said as Patch stood motionless, "there's the little cross pole my mum put up on Saturday, how about a jump over that?" Patch nodded. Joe kicked on. Patch sailed over it. As he did so, Joe's dad arrived at the arena rails. Gyp and Yogi were tumbling over one another, chewing ears and somersaulting in their joy at being reunited, but Patch ignored them and trotted past rhythmically and obediently.

"Looks like you've cracked it," his dad remarked to Joe. Joe grinned. "Will you open the gate dad? I've finished."

"What I don't get is how you can be too ill for school, but not too ill to ride?" Joe didn't answer he was still grinning broadly. His dad whistled to the dogs and strolled towards the house hands deep in pockets.

Joe dismounted, put his arms round Patch's neck, hugged him and whispered. "Thanks sir," in his ear.

"Forget the sir," Patch said. "You and me need to talk." Joe untacked and lead Patch into his stable.

"How about some hay kid?" he asked. Joe thought for a minute. Now wasn't the time to upset him.

"What about carrots instead?" he offered, "they're less fattening." Patch nodded.

Joe returned with half a bucket of carrots and sat down in the straw. "Right", said Patch with his mouth full. "I'll agree to let you ride me for the time you want, including the jumping, provided you'll agree to everything else in my contract. How's that?"

Joe didn't answer, he was busy running through Patch's contract in his head. There were parts of it that he couldn't agree to, but now didn't seem to be the time to say so. Quit while you're ahead, his dad always said. Whilst he was trying to think of an answer that wouldn't cause too much offence, his mum popped her head over the stable door.

"Is that pony eating again?"

"They're only carrots," Joe answered, "they won't do any harm."

"You're right. That's a good idea. I'll get another sack tomorrow. Now, worming", and she held up three syringes of paste. "Will you give me a hand with the foal?" Item four of Patch's contract came to mind and Joe's heart sank.

His mum put Regan's headcollar on, inserted the syringe into the corner of her mouth and quickly squirted its contents onto her tongue. She held Regan's head high, stroked her throat to make her swallow and then gave her a pat. By now Joe had followed his mum into the stable and had put a headcollar on Taz. He held firm, waiting for the explosion, but Taz only threw his head high to avoid the syringe. He wasn't tall enough to get it out of reach, so the paste was in his mouth and down his throat before he had time to complain.

"Right. Patch," his mum announced.

"I'll do Patch," Joe offered, thinking he'd hide the syringe somewhere until he'd had time to discuss it with Patch first.

"No, we've not wormed him before, it might take both of us, you know how awkward he can be."

Yes, thought Joe, I certainly do.

Joe walked in with the head collar and Patch glowered at him. All the time he was fastening it up Joe was talking to Patch, “Now this is for your own good. I know you don't like it but all ponies have to have this, so they don't get ill. If you don’t..." He was still talking when his mum held the syringe up ready for use. Patch shot to the back of the box, dragging Joe with him.

"Hold him there!" his mum shouted, thinking the pony couldn't go back any further. Once more she approached with the syringe. Patch threw his head up. Joe dragged down on the headcollar. Patch went up! He waved his iron shod hooves over Joe's head and as he landed he plunged forwards and kicked backwards at the same time, snorting and blowing. Joe had let go. His mum was talking gently to the pony

"Look at this," she was saying, holding the syringe in front of him and letting him sniff it, "nothing to bother about, is it?" She broke off and turned to Joe, "Go and get your dad."

As Joe ran across the yard he could hear her patiently reassuring Patch. By the time his dad arrived Joe had told him what had happened and was trying to persuade him to leave it until tomorrow. Robert opened the stable door.

"Don't muck about with it. If it's messing, twitch it."

Joe knew that twitching made a pony dozy but Patch had been twitched before. He didn't like it. As the rope approached his top lip, he flung himself against the wall. He kicked out, he reared, he charged the door, and he snorted. Robert backed out.

"Quit while you're ahead," Robert said, "we'll do it tomorrow." Joe's mum sighed. Who was ahead? She hated to be beaten by an animal. Joe on the other hand, was getting used to it.

# CHAPTER SEVEN

Later that evening, Joe offered to take the dogs for a walk. On his way out he picked up the ***Horse and Hound*** from the coffee table and stuffed it in his coat pocket.

"Where are you going with that?" his dad asked. Joe hesitated, he was a bad liar, "I'm going to show some pictures to Patch." His dad looked across the room to his wife. "The kid's flipped," he said. She nodded.

Patch was in one of his moods again. Joe sighed.

"Look Patch. I'm not the boss. My mum and dad are. You sulked on me when you were kept in, but it was my dad who did that, and I didn't decide to give you that medicine, my mum did. Perhaps it's them you should be talking to."

"Grown ups like money. They'd sell me. I'm relying on you to stick up for me. You didn't. You were helping her with that medicine."

"I'm sorry Patch but what else could I do? Eh? What do you think I should have said? ' It says in Patch's ***Terms and Conditions of Employment*** that he won't have medicine?' She'd think I'd gone mad."

"You could have thought of something. People are supposed to be clever." Patch sneered.

Joe sighed and sat down in the straw. He opened ***Horse and Hound*** and pretended to read. Patch moved round to look at the pictures over Joe's shoulder. This was just what Joe had hoped would happen.

"Some time," Patch said, "I wouldn't mind learning to read." Joe grunted, as if in deep thought, "Would you teach me?"

"You must be joking," Joe said. "You're enough trouble as it is." Patch narrowed his eyes, and tilted his head first one way then the other.

"What's that?" he asked.

"What? That?" Joe said innocently. "Oh that's a photograph of the guts of a pony that died of worms."

Patch was silent.

"Yea", Joe went on, "worm eggs are in the grass, but you can't see them. A pony eats the grass and the worms hatch in the pony's guts and eat the pony, from the inside. See these?" (Joe pointed to the photo.) "These are holes where the worms have eaten the eaten the pony's guts away. No wonder it died."

Joe didn't look up, he turned the page and pretended to read the show jumping commentary.

Patch was silent for a long time and then he spoke.

"Are you telling the truth?"

"Why wouldn't I? You've seen the photo."

"So, do you think I have worms in my guts now?"

"I should think so," Joe answered without looking up - he'd learnt that trick from his dad - "you're probably crawling with them. Yep, there will be whole families of them in there, chomping away on your insides, squirming and crawling round.."

"..and that medicine," Patch interrupted, "that kills them does it?"

"What this?" Joe asked, taking the syringe from his pocket. "Yea. It knocks them stone dead." He replaced the syringe and carried on reading. Patch walked away and stood in the middle of the stable.

"All right kid, it's a deal."

Joe stood and was about to put the syringe in the mouth of Patch when he spoke again.

"One day, I'll learn to read and if I find out you've told lies to me, I'll buck you so high that you'll have out grown me by the time you hit the floor. Got it?"

"Got it," said Joe, and he pushed his thumb on he plunger. Patch screwed up his nose and coughed and stamped. "Don't make such a fuss," Joe said, "you've to have some more in six weeks."

When he walked back to the house holding up the empty syringe in triumph, his mum and dad were open mouthed.

"I just explained what would happen if he didn't take it and I showed him this," he said holding up the picture in front of his mum.

"I told you he'd flipped," his dad said. His mum screwed up her eyes. "It's an odd pony," she said. "It's an odd pony."

Joe was feeling much happier about this odd pony Patch was accepting medicine, he didn't want to be called 'sir' any more, he was putting up with a bit of jumping and eating carrots instead of hay without complaining, though he was still too fat.

Over the next few weeks, Joe began to enjoy having such a special pony. They joined Ashley and Bradley for a picnic ride over beautiful Lancashire moor land. They walked for miles, flushing partridges from the heather and stepping between clumps of reeds. Ashley and Bradley were astonished to hear Joe warn his pony of birds about to fly up, or ditches he could see. Bradley tried it with Goldie but she still leapt six inches in the air when a rabbit ran between her legs, and scrambled muddily out of a ditch, even though Bradley had told her it was there. When Joe and Patch were out of earshot, they were able to chat. Patch wanted to know all Joe could tell him about Goldie and Sonny, Ashley's pony. Patch had seemed so bossy and powerful at first but Joe was realising that there was a lot Patch didn't know.

Often, when they could talk safely, Joe would crouch in the straw and answer questions, or listen to Patch's stories of the past. According to Patch, he'd lived through "eleven winters" and had been born somewhere where there were no hills. His mother had been a brown pony with a black mane and she'd pulled a milk float. Until he was four Patch's life had been easy, he'd been kept in a field with a lot of cows and given hay in winter. Then when he was four "the boss" had put his mother in the field and expected Patch to pull the milk float instead.

"Didn't you like that then?" Joe asked. Patch gave him a look of exaggerated patience and then spoke.

"I was harnessed up at four o clock in the morning, everyday, including Sundays. The cart had about 500 bottles of milk on it. In winter the roads hadn't been gritted, they were slippery, so I sometimes fell on my knees. In summer it was hot and I couldn't stop for a drink. I had nothing to protect me against the rain or the flies - would you like it?" Joe shook his head.

"Why did you put up with it?" He was thinking about how stubborn Patch had been about his ***Terms and Conditions of Employment.***

"I was young I suppose," Patch said. "I didn't think I could do anything about it in those days. One morning I had a go, I refused to move, but I just got a stick across my backside. As soon as I moved away from the stick, I pulled the float behind me. So the boss won."

"So why aren't you still delivering milk then?"

"Well, the penny dropped with me eventually. I was lying in the stable one afternoon, knackered as usual, when I thought to myself, if there is no float, I can't pull it, can I? So the next morning, the boss came out at four o clock as usual, put me in the shafts, as usual and before he had time to fasten anything up I just started kicking out with my back legs. You should have heard him shout! I smashed that cart to bits. It was firewood. There was milk, glass, and wood everywhere. The boss just stood there with his mouth open. His teeth dropped out. Remember your mum spotted that scar on my leg the day you first rode me? That's how I got it. The boss got rid of me after that. He got a van."

"Cheeky devil," Joe put in, but he was fascinated by Patch's story. "What then?"

"Well, then a woman in a head scarf came for me, she said I'd make a nice riding pony. I went to her yard where there were many other ponies. I went a long way. I was hungry by the time I got there." You're always hungry, Joe thought, so that doesn't tell me a lot. The white tomcat stretched and slunk from the back of the stable to Joe's knee, as if to get in a more comfortable position from which to listen to the story. Patch lay down in the straw along side them.

"I'd never seen a horse ridden until then so when I saw Monty, a friend of mine from the field, with Head Scarf Woman on his back, I went berserk. I was horrified, I shouted out – oi! Monty! Do you know there's something on your back! - Well, every horse on that yard laughed fit to burst. I never got any rest because as soon as she started riding ***me*** they'd shout –

oi! Young 'un! Do you know there's something on your back!

They thought they were funny. We had a laugh there. If I'd known then what I know now, I'd have stayed there a bit longer. As soon as I was easy to ride, The Head Scarf got rid of me. I should have made her work harder, bucked her off a bit."

Patch sighed. Joe and the cat waited for him to go on.

"Then there was Jemima. The frightful Jemima."

"Was it so bad? Was she cruel to you?" Joe asked.

"Cruel?" Patch repeated, "It was torture. Jemima had seven different colours of hair ribbon, I had seven different velvet brow bands, and all the brow bands had little rose buds at the sides. I had to wear a brow band that matched her ribbons. Sometimes she'd change her ribbons two or three times a day. I had that bridle on and off so often there was no fur behind my ears!

I remember once we were at a show, and her mother was wearing a matching hat and nail polish. Jemima noticed that my brow band was a slightly different shade of pink from her mother's hat. Well, you should have heard the screeching and howling and bawling. When someone is making that racket on your back, you can't get away from it. Anyhow, I had a damned good try. I ran like a steam pig!" Patch laughed as he remembered, "I ran right across the show ground and ended up in the Spillers horse feed tent with my head in a sack of free samples. The kid was still howling though."

Joe knew that cats weren't supposed to laugh but he looked quickly down. He could have sworn the white cat just laughed.

"Could you talk by this time?" Joe asked. Patch thought.

"I could understand," he said, "but I'd never tried talking."

"So, did Jemima get rid of you after that?"

"You're joking. It wasn't that easy. She put up with that sort of thing for years. Every Christmas I was dressed up as the Sugar Plum Fairy, with a frilly tutu round my middle and a tinsel crown on my head..." Joe burst out laughing, he rolled about so much that the cat fell off his knee. Patch stared at him.

"Then the Christmas before last, Jemima wanted me to do a course of show jumps, dressed up as the Sugar Plum Fairy with an audience of a hundred and fifty people and thirty ponies. Well, enough kid, is enough."

"So what did you do?"

"I waited until she was just about to get on and I swung round and grabbed the back of her jacket. I looked her in the face and I said -enough is enough kid. Take me in that ring like this and I'll buck you off so high they'll think you're the fairy on top of the Christmas tree." Joe was holding his sides now and his cheeks were aching from laughing. Patch carried on regardless.

"Do you know what she did? She screamed - Mummy! mummy! I hate this pony! Sell it! Sell it! It's threatening me! - So Mummy sold me to Oak Tree Stables where I bucked off every kid I saw for nearly a year until you came along, and that was only because I was sick of the place, there was no grass left."

"So am I the only other person you've spoken to?" Patch nodded. Joe's mum looked in. She startled Joe, he wondered how long she'd been on the yard.

"Have you been talking to the pony all this time? Come on inside!"

# CHAPTER EIGHT

Carol looked up from the sink.

"You know Robert, Joe's really clicked with that new pony. I was worried at first, but it looks like it might be okay for him. I was wondering if we shouldn't see if he fancies Low Haworth show next week? It's not too far and it's fairly low key." Robert grunted. Joe hesitated when his mother mentioned it.

"I'll let you know," he said. He wanted to discuss it with Patch first.

Patch hesitated.

"No ribbons?"

"No ribbons."

"No velvet brow bands?"

"No velvet brow bands, and no Sugar Plum Fairies." Patch nodded.

Most ponies of Patch's age behave well at shows. They've done it before and they know what to expect. With Patch though, it was possible to explain it all in advance, even down to the timing of his classes and the route to the show ground. So when Joe's dad lowered the ramp of the trailer at Low Haworth agricultural show, Patch backed slowly out and stood looking around munching his last mouthful of hay.

Their first class was the clear round at half past nine. Joe spoke to Patch.

"Okay Patch, I'll go and look at the course, you stay here." He flung the lead rope over the pony's back and walked towards the ring. Patch put his head down and started to graze.

"Oi! You can't do that! Tie him up!" Joe's dad shouted after him. Joe's mum climbed out of the Land Rover.

"He does that all the time at home," she said, "he'll be okay."

"Carol! Are you nuts as well? You can't leave a pony loose on a show ground."

"No, I suppose not," she answered. "He's not like other ponies, so I sometimes forget." She tied Patch to the trailer.

Joe was already in ring one and walking the course. It was straight forward apart from the last double. There was nothing higher than about forty five centimetres. He collected the number for his jacket from the secretary's tent and strode back to Patch.

"Easy peesy lemon squeezy!" he announced to the pony. "The first fence is at the other side of the ring from where you come in. It's green. Then it's the yellow cross pole, the black and white upright and then the gate, the planks, a red oxer, and a double going away from the horse box lines to finish. The highest is up to your hock." Joe was brushing Patch as he was speaking and Patch nodded as if taking it in.

Joe's mum watched Joe suspiciously, "You never talked to Fudge like that."

"It calms my nerves," Joe said.

"Nerves?" Joe's dad scoffed, "You don't know what nerves are, either of you. You're damned near asleep most of the time." Joe carried on brushing.

"The pony was nodding," Joe's mum said, "like it understood." His dad looked at her, his eyes narrowed.

"They all nod," he said. "Ponies nod."

Joe tacked up, mounted and rode to the collecting ring. At the edge of the ring, his mum handed him a stick. Joe shook his head.

"Take it!" his dad said. "You might need it!" Joe rode away. "Well jump the practice fence then!" he yelled.

"Do you want to?" Joe whispered to Patch

"No, I don't. There's enough jumping to do in there." Joe grinned, "No!" he shouted back at his dad.

"Cheeky beggar! He knows it all doesn't he? He deserves to have them all down."

Joe heard the announcement he was waiting for over the PA system

**"...and the next pair in the ring are number 127 Joseph Cooper and Patch..."**

They trotted in confidently and circled until they heard the bell. Patch trotted forward and popped every fence with ease. He rattled the back rail of the double, but it stayed in place. It was exactly as Joe hoped it would be and, grinning, he accepted his clear round rosette from the steward as he left the ring.

"Well done!" he said and he hugged the pony's neck.

"Whew!" Patch complained, "I'm knackered."

"What?" the steward said to Joe, "The day's only just started." Joe smiled and trotted Patch away.

"That was close," Joe said, "that steward heard you!" Patch laughed. Knackered or not, their next class was junior equitation. Joe took Patch aside and explained it to him.

"Right," he said, "in here, keep your head down and when you move, pull your legs well underneath you. I'll just sit straight and still, so you'll have to listen to what I say to you. I'll whisper. Okay?" Patch nodded.

In the ring, Joe and Patch were the third pair to go. The judge looked carefully for any kicking or flapping from the rider's legs. Nothing. This child rode so well she couldn't even see what he was doing! And the pony! He held his head in a beautiful position with hardly any contact down the reins. She just had to place them first. She watched the next seven ponies just as carefully, but none were anything like as good as number 127.

Joe heard the crackle of the tannoy again, **"...and the result of the junior equitation class: first number 127 Joseph Cooper, second..."**

But Joe and Patch were looking happily at the clapping crowd and didn't listen to the rest. They rode their lap of honour at a furious gallop but as soon as they were out of the ring Patch stopped dead and gasped for air.

"I hope that's it," he said.

"Afraid not," Joe's mum said from behind him. "You've the 12.2 jumping to do yet." She leaned over and kissed Joe on the cheek. "Well done love."

"You did it again !" Joe hissed, laughing, when his mum was out of earshot. "You're getting careless!"

His third class the 12.2 and under jumping was over the same course as the clear round, but all the fences had been put up a few centimetres. Patch groaned as Joe explained this.

"You can do it!" Joe encouraged him as they trotted into the ring, "Make it three out of three!"

The bell rang and they popped over the first cross pole, no trouble. The black and white upright was okay too, though they got a bit close to the gate. They cantered on to the planks, which looked a lot bigger than they had earlier, and Patch rattled the top plank. Joe looked over his shoulder to check it hadn't fallen.

As they approached the oxer Patch was beginning to puff and pant, and by the time they reached the first part of the double, he'd dropped back to a trot.

Joe shouted at him

"Canter!" This drew a laugh from the crowd and Patch managed three laboured canter strides but by the time he'd landed after the first part of the double he didn't have enough bounce left to get over the second. He stopped. Joe sighed. He turned Patch away from the fence and rode to the middle of the ring.

"Patch," he said, "do these two and we can go home."

"Okay," Patch panted, between breaths. He struck off in canter once again and after his brief rest cleared the first part again, but caught the top rail of the second part with a back foot. It fell. Joe patted Patch.

The tannoy crackled again, **"That's seven faults for number 127, Joseph Cooper and Patch."**

Joe's mum was waiting at the ringside; she patted Patch's neck.

"Well ridden Joe."

"He'd do better if he had a stick," Joe's dad added. "If you'd had a stick he'd have been over that last fence."

"He wouldn't dad, he was knackered."

"Well get some more weight off the fat thing then!"

"It doesn't work," Joe's mum insisted, "I'll swear that pony gets fat off fresh air. If it has no hay it just eats its straw bedding."

Although he was out of the 12.2 jumping Joe was happy with their first outing. He realised his dad was right though - not about the stick, about the fat. If Patch was going to do more shows, he needed to be slimmer, as it was he couldn't keep going all day. He also needed more work at home to get him fitter.

An idea was already brewing in his head.

# CHAPTER NINE.

Over the next few days Joe dragged down from the shelves every book he could find about horses. His dad had loads of them, ***"Veterinary Notes for the Horse Owner", "The Horse Care Handbook", "Foals and Foaling"*** (he put that back), ***"Training the Young Horse"*** (that was no use either), ***"Training the Event Horse", "The Cross Country Manual."*** He piled them up, hauled them all upstairs and dumped them on his bed. He took a pencil and sitting at his desk he went carefully through each of them, underlining useful passages.

Joe's dad walked in.

"What're you doing son?"

"Reading," Joe answered "about getting a pony fit."

"Good lad!" his dad said, ruffling his hair. He was pleased that his son was taking his hobby seriously. He'd been the same at Joe's age, or a little older. Perhaps they should have saved up and bought him a better pony? He was even enjoying caring for the horses these days. More often than not it was Joe who gave them their last feed at night.

So it was that night. His pocket crammed with ***The Horse Care Handbook*** Joe set off for the yard. His dad would have psyched if he'd known he'd taken it outside. The book was fat and heavy and weighed his coat down so Joe had been careful to hide it in the wash room before it was time to go out, so as not to arouse suspicion.

After he'd fed Regan and Taz and walked the dogs, he gathered up an armful of hay for Patch, put it in his rack, walked casually up to him and stroked his neck.

"Did you enjoy the show on Sunday?"

"Yea, it was a change," Patch answered, "I'd prefer just to do one class though, I'm getting too old."

"Nonsense," said Joe, "if you lost some more weight, you'd be able to keep going all day. Listen..." and he took out the book. ***"The responsible owner does not allow his horse or pony to become obese. The normal respiratory rate for a horse or pony is 10 to 14 breaths per minute, but obesity can greatly increase this rate, making exercise both difficult and dangerous."*** He flicked furiously through the pages and began again, ***"Obesity in the horse or pony is a major factor in the cause of heart failure."*** Patch looked at him

"What's obesity?" he said. Joe sighed.

"Fatness! It's saying that fat ponies get out of breath and die of heart disease."

"I'm not fat," Patch said.

"No, you're not. You're disgustingly gross."

Patch stared at Joe, insulted. "Listen to it again," Joe said, and he read once more. There was a pause whilst Patch chewed.

"What's respiratory rate?"

"Breathing! How fast you breathe!" There was another pause.

"What's factor?"

"It doesn't matter."

"You've made it up."

"I couldn't make that up, I didn't know the words until I read them!" Patch stared at him and sighed a deep horse sigh.

"I wish I could read."

"Think about it," Joe said and he put the closed book under his arm. Just as he was about to unbolt the door, he turned. "Have you got enough hay there Patch? Or would you like a bit more?"

"Get lost," Patch said sulkily.

Patch was still quiet when Joe went in the next morning before school. He pulled ***The Horse Care Handbook*** from his school bag as Patch was eating his carrots. Patch looked up. Joe grinned and started reading again, ***"feed according to exercise. Increase the amount of concentrated food, (oats etc.) if the demands of work are heavy."*** Patch stopped, mid munch.

"Does that mean if I do more work I can have more food?"

"Yep!" Joe said, "It works like this: You eat less hay but do more work, then you get more oats, mix, and stuff."

"How much more?" Patch asked, looking for the catch.

"Only a bit at first but the book says you'll find work easier and want to do more when you're fitter, and you'll get fitter by doing what it says."

"I wish I could read," Patch said, and carried on eating.

"Well?"

Patch sighed a rib-heaving sigh.

"We'll give it a go, kid."

It was only when he said it that Joe realised he hardly ever called him kid any more.

"Mum!" he called out in the direction of the house as he ran out to catch the school bus, "I want to ride when I get home, so keep Patch in."

Joe rode almost every day that week. On Monday he went for a quiet hack around the farm, on Tuesday they did flatwork on the arena, on Wednesday they did some jumping, (even though it was raining), on Thursday they rode out with Bradley and Goldie and on Friday they had a day off.

"Mum," Joe said on Saturday morning as he groomed Patch for yet another ride, "don't you think we should give Patch some more coarse mix? He's doing a lot more work and he gets out of puff." Patch's ears pricked forward.

"You'll have to drop his hay."

"I've dropped it." His mum stood back and looked at Patch from every angle.

"See how he goes on a full scoop of that mix."

Patch nodded vigorously, he was only on half a scoop at the moment. "I'll swear that pony understands every word we say!" she laughed. Patch winked at her. Not the quick blink of an eye, but the slow deliberate wink of one who knows.

"I wish it wouldn't do that though," she said, "it makes me go all shivery." This time it was Joe who laughed and Patch curled his top lip with him

"I don't know how you put up with it Joe, except that it's as daft as you are," and she strolled away.

Patch lost weight, his coat gleamed when it caught the sun, the muscles on his chest and haunches stood out and he was on two scoops of mix a day. For the first time since he'd come to them, nearly five months ago, he really wanted to work. Actually it was the first time in his life he'd wanted to work. He felt well and there were days when he had more energy than he could use up without effort. Then he'd buck and plunge around the field just like he had as a foal. He found that it was possible to buck for fun, not just as a means of ditching a rider. Now Patch was fit, Joe sometimes rode him to the bottom of the gently sloping meadow in order to canter him back up again. Their canters often became gallops nowadays and Patch was impatient to start them. He'd try to swing round before they'd reached the bottom and sometimes he'd do it so fast, Joe dropped off sideways.

"You Wally!" Joe had shouted the last time he did it.

"Get up you dope!" Patch drawled. When Joe was on board Patch jumped and bucked for the joy of it. "Hold on to your teeth kid!" (Patch was convinced that all people had removable teeth since his bosses had fallen out when he'd smashed the milk float all those years ago.)Then he'd pogo up and down, like one of the mechanical bulls Joe's dad had ridden at the fair. "It's not funny you maniac!" Joe squealed, but he was laughing at the same time.

Nowadays, he walked home after his ride, sweating, glowing and ravenously hungry. If it had rained, he'd be spattered with mud too. Joe had never been more delighted with a pony. They'd been to four more shows, won ten more rosettes and a trophy for junior open jumping.

"You've done wonders with that pony Carol," Bradley's mum had said at the ringside as Joe received his trophy.

"I haven't Linda, it's Joe," Carol admitted, "I can't get on with that pony at all. Nobody can. Only Joe."

"Bradley says he's forever talking to it."

"He is, he talks to it more than he talks to me. He reads it flaming magazines. Takes ***Horse and***

***Hound*** out to it would you believe?" Linda burst into laughter.

"Daft little devil!" she said, as Bradley and Goldie received their rosette for second place.

*"**The Horse Care Handbook*** as well. He thinks we don't know. He takes ***The Horse Care Handbook*** out and he reads bits out to it, I've heard him. Then he puts a deep voice on, like it's answering back."

"It's not normal isn't that!" Linda said, laughing.

# CHAPTER TEN

Patch had done so well that they planned to take him to the Great Ulverton Show to finish the season off. It was two hour's drive away, but Joe desperately wanted to go there. Great Ulverton was where all the best ponies went. He'd never had a pony good enough to take there before, so this year was special. Joe couldn't help a sly grin when he remembered how Ashley had laughed at Patch a few months ago. His grin broadened when he remembered how he'd replied!

Great Ulverton Show was as grand as Joe remembered it. There was a bandstand decked in ribbons and flowers. A brass band of uniformed men and women, their cheeks puffed out like hamsters, loudly played well known tunes. A crowd of people seemed to have gone to the show just to hear the band. They were settled comfortably on fold down aluminium chairs or shooting sticks and they tapped their feet and sang along nodding their heads between mouthfuls of hot dog or ice cream. Behind the bandstand were caravans with counters cut into their sides, selling sweets and bacon rolls, crepe suzettes and cups of tea, beer and freshly squeezed lemonade. There were rows and rows of tents, selling everything from waxed jackets to designer pullovers, from original paintings to hand made jewellery. Joe spotted a

Spillers horse feed tent and laughed aloud as he remembered Patch's story of how he'd once ended up in there.

Joe walked down the horse box lines in search of the secretary's tent from where he was to collect his number. He wove between the stands, stopped for a hot dog at a caravan (there was plenty of time) and listened to the band play the theme from EastEnders whilst he ate it. There were three big rings, each with a temporary grandstand next to it for spectators to get a good view. Joe walked on, past the pens of bleating sheep, past smells of poultry and snuffles of pigs, through the deep grumbling and lowing of cows who'd rather be in the field, all handled by burly men in white coats. He found the secretary's tent and realised he'd walked a circle of the show ground and was only a hundred yards from the trailer!

He looked at his number, 548, folded it and slipped it into his pocket. As he took the schedule out to see which ring he was in, he noticed he'd managed to get tomato sauce on his jacket. He hoped his mum wouldn't notice. He spat on his finger and rubbed it. It would have to do. He was so busy scrubbing at his jacket that he almost failed to notice the heavy horses on their way into the ring. He loved to watch them. Their feet moving in high graceful arcs over the ground, the white feather above their great hooves, flowing with the movement. Their vast heads held low, arching powerful necks which were decked with ribbons of yellow and green or red and blue. Even Patch couldn't have thought ***they*** looked sissy. On their backs were arches of ribbons and flowers, hung with bells that jangled at every movement. Their tails were short and plaited, sprouting ribbons of the same colours as those in their manes. Their harnesses sparkled in the morning sun.

Joe thought he'd like to have a shire horse one day, (if he didn't become a show-jumper, or a jockey, or a racehorse trainer, or a stud manager.) Despite the fact that this was the biggest show he'd ridden at, he wasn't in the least nervous. Patch wasn't the unknown quantity that Fudge had been. Even at little shows, Joe had been nervous with Fudge. He hadn't minded the nervousness. In fact, he quite missed the fizz it made in his tummy.

"We haven't all week you know," his dad said as Joe ambled back to the trailer. "You're in the ring in three quarters of an hour and you haven't even tacked up yet."

"No sweat," Joe remarked and proceeded to brush Patch down. His mum had been on the stable yard since five that morning, first shampooing Patch, then plaiting his mane and tail. Joe and his dad had managed to persuade her to forget the ribbons. Plaited up and fit, Patch looked magnificent.

Joe tacked up, mounted and rode for the collecting ring. "What's that on your jacket?" his mum asked. Joe pretended he hadn't heard and kicked on

In the collecting ring they trotted and cantered a few circles and unlike in the old days, Patch was raring to jump the practice fence, even though they weren't in a jumping competition today. They jumped it at a foot and again at eighteen inches and again at two foot six. Each time Patch cleared the fence easily, his ears pricked. They turned the corner at canter for yet another approach - Patch suddenly planted both front feet firmly in the turf and stopped in his tracks. Joe shot forward and slumped across Patch's neck.

"Wally!" Joe shouted. "What was that for?"

Patch didn't move. He didn't speak. As Joe manoeuvred himself back into the saddle, Patch remained stock still, staring ahead. Joe was beginning to feel concerned.

"Patch? Patch?" he said, "What's up?" Patch shook his head until his ears flapped and seemed to partly return to his senses.

"There," Patch said, "in front."

In front of them walking into the ring were a girl of about Joe's age and her pony, a pretty little bay mare.

"Those two?" Joe asked, still not following this at all Patch still hadn't moved and Joe noticed that he was breathing quick shallow breaths, like Fudge used to when he saw a water jump. Joe looked again at the pair who had just entered the ring. The girl was very pretty and her white blonde hair was worn in two long plaits on either side of her head. Each plait was tied with a pink ribbon. She wore a pink rose-bud in the lapel of her black jacket and her pony wore a pink and burgundy velvet brow band, trimmed with pink rose buds.

"Jemima," Patch said. "Jemima." He hung his head.

"Of course!" Joe shrieked, "I should have known!"

"I can't go I," Patch said.

"Yes you can!" Joe urged. "You can show her what she's missing! We'll keep down this end until it's time to go in."

But Patch had lost all his spark. All the fun had gone. There was no joy in it now

Suddenly, there was a piercing wail from the other side of the ring. "Mummy! Mummy! It's that pony! It's Puddington Podge!"

A woman in a large navy blue hat with a pink band, and wearing a navy blue suit with a pink rose in the lapel, raised her hand and wafted pink painted nails in the direction of her daughter.

"Nonsense darling. What would Puddington Podge be doing here? He's ***hardly*** up to this standard!"

"Mummy, it's him, I know it!" Jemima pointed a long finger in the direction of Joe and Patch. Joe was too busy giggling to be worried by Jemima's witchy finger!

"Puddington Podge! Puddington Podge! What a name!" he snorted.

"Jemima dear, that pony has been ***flying*** over the practice fence. Podge couldn't do that."

"Mummy, I know it! The boy is talking to it! See!"

"Oh I do hope we're not going to start all that nonsense again Jemima. I haven't brought your tablets. Now don't get so excited, Jemima. That pony isn't even fat." But Jemima had burst into tears and was sobbing and wailing all over her pony's neck.

"She's off," Patch said. "Once she starts there's no stopping her." As he spoke, Mummy strode purposefully into the ring, and straight up to Joe.

"Excuse me dear," she began, "your pony has upset my daughter, could you keep it away from her please?" Before Joe could answer, his mum was in the ring.

"Is there a problem?"

"Well, its rather awkward," Jemima's mother answered, embarrassed, "my daughter has been ... ill" She hesitated - "You see, she became convinced that a pony she'd had for ***years*** suddenly spoke to her. She's had treatment of course, and she's getting better, but this pony of your son's looks a little like it, and it's upset her - and I haven't brought her tablets."

Joe saw the colour drain from his mother's face.

"We'll do what we can to help, obviously, but if they're in the same ring together we can't allow for where the judge places them, can we?" Jemima's mother hesitated again,

"- I don't suppose we could persuade you not to go into the ring could we? If it's a question of money, there is no problem. My husband is a *very* wealthy man..."

Joe's mum was already walking away. What a cheek the woman had! Did she think they'd travelled all this way to let a hysterical little girl keep them out of the competition?

Joe continued to work Patch in, but he was worried about him. When Patch was far enough from the other ponies he finally spoke. "I'll show them!" he said.

"Yes!" Joe hissed, "we'll show them."

The tannoy crackled **...will the competitors for class three, the First Ridden Pony, please make their way to ring one..."**

Jemima was first in the ring, still snivelling as Patch had predicted. As Joe rode in a few moments later he could hear Jemima's mother from the ring side.

"Pull yourself together Jemima! Don't you dare make a spectacle of yourself! Ignore that pony. It isn't fat enough to be Podge." Joe felt Patch breathe in sharply. He arched his neck, drew his hind legs underneath him and trotted around that ring as if it were Wembley. Joe smiled. Jemima's mum had done him a favour.

Jemima rode well, apart from occasionally altering her position to wipe the tears from her eyes with her sleeve. She looked like serious competition. Her pony was a light framed delicate little animal that carried herself well. She had the fragile twig like legs of a deer and beautiful, wet, round brown eyes.

When it was the turn of Joe and Patch, Joe could hear Jemima begin to sniff, and for a brief moment, he felt sorry for her. He remembered how miserable he'd been when Patch first spoke to him and how he too had been afraid. Patch had no such sympathy. All he had in mind were the years and years of velvet brow bands. The fact that Joe wasn't concentrating didn't affect their performance at all. Joe just had to sit still, Patch knew the routine by heart.

When all the ponies had gone, the judge stood and spoke to the steward for a moment. The steward had a clipboard in her hand and the judge looked at it, and considered and pointed to it, then walked away. She looked Joe in the eye and pointed to him. Joe grinned and rode to the middle of the ring. The judge then pointed to Jemima, who was expected to ride into place next to him. Instead, she left a huge space. The judge indicated that Jemima should move nearer. Not really wanting to, she did so. Patch did not flicker, he did not turn. Joe turned and smiled at Jemima.

Very often the child who's come second will congratulate the one who's come first. Whenever Joe was second, he did that. Jemima simply stared back and said, "I don't like your pony." Joe didn't know what to say, so he said nothing. He'd like to have said, 'well I don't like yours', but he couldn't, because he did. "My mum says its not Puddington Podge, but I know it is. I don't know how the thing has beaten me." Joe still didn't answer, he wasn't used to such open rudeness. "It talks doesn't it?" Jemima said, as she looked him in the eye.

"I sometimes wish it didn't," Joe answered. The judge approached him with his rosette. Joe shook her hand and thanked her. By the time Jemima was presented with her rosette, she was crying again.

The tannoy crackled, "**The results of the First Ridden Pony class: first, Joseph Cooper and Patch.**

**Second, Jemima Pearce-Jones and Kisscandy Cupcake."**

Joe was laughing again.

"That poor pony," he exclaimed to his mum as he left the ring, "what a name!" Joe's dad walked up, "Good lad Joe!" he said and patted him hard on the back. It was a sticky day and Patch had got all hot and steamy with the work and the worry, so Joe was sponging him down at the trailer when he heard a voice behind him.

"How d'y do. Pearce-Jones is the name." Joe turned and saw a fleshy man with a bald head shaking hands with his dad. "I just watched your son win the First Ridden Pony. Splendid. Splendid. Topping little pony."

"Thanks," Joe's dad answered, puzzled as to what all this was about.

"I'll get to the point," said Pearce-Jones. "I've not become the success I am in business by beating about the bush," and he grinned to show a line of yellow teeth. "My daughter, she's not been a well girl, not well at all you see, ... not physical, you understand, ... if you see what I mean ...? and what she needs is to build up her confidence, you see." Joe's dad couldn't see what this had to do with him. "That pony of yours, it's a winner! Do her confidence the world of good. I'd like to buy it. Name your price!" As he spoke, he pulled a fat cheque book from his pocket. Two voices rang out at the same time.

"Dad!"

"Nigel!"

Joe had stopped sponging Patch and was staring at his father, who suddenly seemed to him like a cartoon character with dollar signs instead of pupils. Mrs Pearce-Jones had run to her husband. "What are you doing?" she demanded.

"Buying this pony for Mima," her husband explained.

"Darling," said Mrs Pearce-Jones, through gritted teeth, "Jemima doesn't want that pony. She doesn't like that pony. She's been crying all afternoon ***because*** of that pony. She says it's Podge."

Nigel Pearce-Jones had put his cheque book back in his pocket and a cigar in his mouth. He took the cigar out in order to laugh at his wife's last remark.

"Podge!" he exclaimed, ***"That? I*** know my Mima, and the only reason she's crying is that she's been beaten." Mrs Pearce-Jones took hold of her husband's hand to lead him away. "Women eh?" he shrugged, in the direction of Joe's dad, and handed him a card. "My card," he said. "Give me a ring in a day or two, when I've sorted out the little woman. Just name your price."

Joe's mum had been sitting on the tailgate. It wasn't like her not to interfere, but she'd resisted the temptation. Joe went and sat next to her.

"Dad won't sell Patch, will he?"

"He's not his to sell."

"But he won't? Will he?"

"No love," she said, and she hugged him. "Not if you don't want him to. I'll make sure he doesn't."

"Patch doesn't want to go back to those people."

His mum removed her arm from around Joe's shoulders and turned to face him.

"What are you talking about?"

Joe bit his lip.

"Did that girl own him?" Joe nodded. "How do you know?" Joe didn't speak. "You can't go off what the girl says. She's ... confused. You know?"

"I know," Joe said.

"So what's going on? What are you talking about?"

“There are some things I just ***know*** with Patch mum. I just know them." (It wasn't a lie. Joe hadn't said how he knew them.)

"That girl said her pony spoke to her you know?" Joe nodded again. "You said yourself, she's - confused" he answered.

His mum sighed. She took a swig from the coke can by her side, then sat with it between her knees as she thought of the way the pony winked and curled its lips and nodded, and of the deep voice she'd heard Joe use in the stable with it. Perhaps Jemima wasn't the only one who was confused? Perhaps Bradley's mum was right about Joe? Perhaps they'd be better off without that pony?

Joe received his trophy in the grand parade and had his photograph taken for the Great Ulverton Observer. It seemed right that a fierce summer storm broke out whilst they were in the ring. This should have been a brilliant day but Joe felt that it had been spoilt. When he returned, soaked, to the trailer Joe's dad was waiting with a rug for Patch. As his dad loaded the pony Joe dragged his old kagoul from the back of the Land Rover.

"Where's your mum?" his dad asked, irritated at having to sort the pony out alone. Joe pointed.

There in the rain, his mother was holding a plastic bag over her head whilst talking to a soggy Mrs Pearce-Jones. She'd walked along the horse box lines until she'd found a pink and white Mercedes lorry with ***Jemima Pearce-Jones*** painted on the side of it in flowery writing. Joe wasn't near enough to hear the conversation, which was probably just as well.

"You said that Jemima thought her old pony could talk?" Carol was saying.

"I shouldn’t have said anything," Mrs Pearce-Jones answered, "I don't want her to be a laughing stock. My daughter is ill. She's having treatment. The last thing she needs is to have people like you laugh at her."

"I'm not laughing at her Mrs Pearce-Jones, believe me," and she put a reassuring hand on the other woman's arm. "The truth is, I'm worried about my son. He's not said his pony talks, but I'm sure he believes it does. I think he might have a similar problem."

"You poor thing! I can't tell you how awful it's been for the whole family," Mrs Pearce-Jones said. "Still, we found a splendid doctor. I could give you his address, and Jemima did seem to be on the mend until today, when she saw that pony - " She stopped.

"What did you do with Podge in the end Mrs Pearce-Jones?" Carol finally asked.

"We sold him to a dealer in Dorrington. Oak Tree Stables I think they called the place." Carol stared at her, "Oh my God," was all she said.

# CHAPTER ELEVEN.

Joe caught a cold at Great Ulverton show. The soaking he got at the end of the day put him in bed for a week. His mum insisted he stayed in bed although he made three attempts to put on his jeans and go outside. "Patch will be wondering where I am!" Joe exclaimed, desperate for his mother to understand.

"He's all right, he's having a few days well deserved rest. He's out in the field with Regan and Taz."

"Will you explain to him that I'm ill?"

"Joe!" his mum shouted. "I'm sick of all this damned nonsense! It's a ***pony!"*** Joe was shocked at his mother's sudden outburst. "Please?" he said weakly as his mother tucked him in again. She bent and kissed his hot forehead, but she didn't answer him. "Dad hasn't phoned those people, has he?" he asked.

"No love," his mum answered.

Downstairs Joe's dad had ***The Farmer's Guardian*** in front of his face.

"Robert," Carol said sharply, "I'm worried about that child.".

"It's only bad cold," Robert answered, his face still behind the paper.

"Will you put that flaming paper down and listen to me for once!" Robert lowered the paper, surprised that his wife seemed so agitated. "I'm not talking about his cold. It's this nonsense with the pony, reading to it, pretending it can talk, all that. It's getting beyond a joke." Robert sighed. Carol went on, "I think it might be better if we did get rid of it after all." Robert raised his eyebrows.

"I thought you were on his side?"

"I am," Carol said, "but sometimes you have to be cruel to be kind. I don't want him on tablets and everyone thinking he's nuts, like that poor Pearce-Jones kid. We can buy him another pony."

"He'd just do the same with another."

"He wouldn't," Carol answered firmly, "it's ***this*** pony. I'm telling you. There's something not right." Robert had had enough of this. He stood up, folded the paper and left the room.

Carol sighed, but she set up the ironing board and plugged in the iron as she'd intended to, despite the lump in her throat that meant she couldn't swallow. She knew that selling Patch would devastate Joe. She put the washing basket on the table, then remembered a T-shirt of Joe's that was drying on the radiator at the foot of the stairs. She walked into the hall, and to her horror heard the beginnings of a telephone conversation.

"Mr Pearce-Jones? Robert Cooper here, we met at..." and Carol put her fingers on the two black buttons where the receiver goes. Robert swung round.

"What was that for? Eh? We could get five thousand pounds for that pony! You just said we should sell it! Five thousand pounds would fence the meadow and buy a half decent car for you!"

A noise made Robert turn swiftly. He saw Joe sitting on the top step of the stairs with his head in his hands and his shoulders shaking in great heaving sobs. His dad looked from Joe to Carol and back again.

"I give up!" he exclaimed, grabbed his jacket from the coat stand, and slammed out.

Joe's mum began to climb the stairs.

"Get lost!" Joe shouted, still sobbing. He ran thundering to his room, banged the door shut in his mother's face and threw himself on the bed crying inconsolably.

"Joe..." his mother attempted. Joe turned a red stained, wet eyed, tear streaked and angry face to her.

"Get out!" he yelled. "You get out of my room! Selling that pony was your idea! Dad said it! Get out!"

His mum knew there would be no reasoning with him now. She gently closed the door.

Joe had never felt so desperate, helpless and misunderstood in all his life. He cried and heaved so that he struggled to breathe between sobs. His eyes and nose ran with hot tears and snot. His pillow and duvet were chill and wet to his cheeks. In his stomach he felt heavy and cold.

After a long time the crying gradually stopped. His eyelids felt scratchy and puffy. He wiped the remaining tears away roughly with his hands. He sat on is bed and gazed through his window at the farmyard. He watched two large Aylesbury drakes splash about in the puddle left by the tyres of the Land Rover. He sighed a deep desperate sigh.

His mum meanwhile was trying to do the ironing, but tears were blurring her vision. She blinked and brushed them away but each time her eyes filled up with them again until they over flowed and ran down her hot cheeks. It was useless. She switched the iron off and threw herself in an armchair. She hated upsetting Joe like this. She knew that he must feel betrayed. She'd told him she'd make sure his dad didn't sell Patch. She remembered how grown-ups had done things like that to her when she was a little girl. She remembered how her mum had said she could have a bike if she passed her eleven plus and how much she hated her when no bike ever came. She remembered how she'd promised herself she'd never do that if she had a child of her own. She was a rotten mother. She'd done it all wrong. - And yet how mad would Joe end up if she let him ***keep*** that odd pony? She hated the day she'd ever bought it. She wished she'd never clapped eyes on it.

She wiped her eyes. She couldn't hear Joe's sobs any more. Perhaps he'd calmed down? She stood up and walked quietly upstairs, aware of every creaking step. She tapped quietly on Joe's door.

"Can I come in? Please Joe, I want to talk to you."

"Well I don't want to talk to you. Not ever again." She pushed the door open a crack.

"Please Joe?" Joe was still staring out of the window, he didn't turn. His mum came in and sat on the bedside chair. "Joe," she began, "I'm worried about you. Patch ***is*** Jemima's old pony you know."

***"I*** told ***you*** that," Joe said with his back to her. His mum remained patient.

"Jemima's mum told me what happened to Jemima, and how she's had to see a psychiatrist because she said the pony could talk."

"So?" Joe said, turning his head for the first time.

"Well, I know you pretend it talks, I've heard you - and you read to it."

"I've never said it talks."

"No, but you ***think*** it does, don't you?" Joe was silent for a moment. ***"You*** think it winks at you," he said. His mum nodded.

"So, you do think it talks then?"

Joe stared out of the window fixedly. He'd told Patch he wouldn't say anything. 'No telling', they'd agreed - but everything had changed since then. Patch had been afraid that if Joe's mum and dad knew he could talk they'd sell him, but here they were about to sell him anyway. What did he have to lose?

"Well?" his mother persisted. Joe was still thinking. At the moment his mum thought he was nuts. He turned to her. She was still staring at him. If she knew the truth -? He took a breath.

"I don't ***think*** he talks mum, I ***know*** he does."

She continued to stare at him, just as before at first, then her eyes began to search Joe's face for some clue that he was joking, just winding her up. There was no such clue. She hung her head and a tear dropped from her eye onto Joe's Blackburn Rovers duvet cover.

“Mum?" Joe asked gently, not sure as to why she was crying.

"Never mind," she said, sniffing and brushing her eyes, "never mind," and she left the room shaking her head.

Joe realised that in telling his mum he'd not only betrayed Patch, he'd also confirmed all his mum's fears. She didn't ***think*** he was nuts any more, she ***knew*** he was nuts.

There was nothing else for it, he would have to explain it all to Patch. That wouldn't be easy either. His mum certainly wouldn't let him go out and see Patch now, even if he managed to convince her he was well enough. He couldn't waste time either, it they were going to sell him, he'd sell quickly as a championship winner.

As he continued to stare out of the window Joe saw his dad's Land Rover drive into the yard. The

Aylesbury drakes flew up in a flap of white feathers as he trundled to his usual parking spot. His dad locked the door, whistled for the dogs and disappeared round the corner with them lolloping at his heels. He'd gone to bring he horses in.

Joe began to brew a plan in his head. He would have to sneak out after dark. He'd wait until everyone was in bed, then he'd sneak out to the stables. The creaking stairs would be a problem, and he'd have to move about by the key-ring light that he kept attached to his jeans. He thought it through. He'd set his radio alarm for three o'clock in the morning. He'd set the volume low, but place it right next to his pillow. He'd push his tracksuit under the bed so it was out of the way but easy to grab and pull on in the dark. He'd need something to keep the dogs quiet. Dog chews! He'd put two dog chews in his pocket to stop the dogs whining after him when he'd gone out. He needed to be organised. He decided to sleep for a bit now if he could, so that he wouldn't be too tired at three in the morning. He still didn't feel completely well. He switched on his electric over blanket, that usually made him feel drowsy.

# CHAPTER TWELVE

When he next looked at his clock it was ten thirty. He could hear the muffled murmurs of his mum and dad's voices as they made their way to bed. He'd slept for three hours. He frowned as he lay there. He remembered that once he'd woken up wishing none of it were true. He'd wished for an ordinary pony. Now the last thing in the world he wanted was an ordinary pony. In these past few months, Patch had become his best friend.

He waited until the creak of floorboards and the rumble of opening drawers had stopped and then he crept out of bed, positioned his tracksuit and his radio alarm as planned. He took a felt tipped pen and wrote DOG CHEWS, as best he could by the light of the key-ring, on the back of an old birthday card, and propped the card on his bedside chair. He slipped on a pair of socks and left his trainers at the foot of his bed. He opened his bedroom door so his mum and dad wouldn't hear the click of the handle later on. He waited. All was quiet. He was all set.

At 3.04 he became dimly aware of a male voice in his left ear. ***...fm and stereo. This one is especially for all you truckers out there, riding the highways at the dead of night...*** Joe leaned over and switched it off. This was it. If he blew it now, they would be convinced he was ready for the mad house. He raised his eyes to the ceiling, clasped his hands and pleaded.

"Please, please, let me not get caught." He wasn't certain who he was pleading to. He only ever prayed in school, but just now, it seemed necessary.

He wriggled into his tracksuit and stuffed his special key-ring into his pocket. He untied his trainers and put them on, usually he would have forced his foot into them without bothering about the laces, but he was afraid his heel might bang down on the floor. He walked stealthily to his door and tiptoed down stairs. The third step creaked so violently, the groan of it seemed to penetrate every corner of the house. Joe froze. He lowered himself onto his bottom. He waited. Nothing. He shuffled the rest of the steps on his bottom. He stood and listened. Still silent. He crossed the hall to the living room door. Good, they'd left it open. He crossed the carpet, quiet as a cat, and put his hand on the kitchen door. He paused. He remembered that this door usually opened with a noisy crack. His mum and dad's room was directly above. He took a deep breath, pulled the door as hard as he could toward him and turned the handle. There was a slight click. Joe sighed with relief. He'd have to return that way, so he left the door ajar.

Now, the dogs. He crept across the kitchen and gently opened the cupboard under the sink. By the light of his key-ring he rifled about amongst bottles of bleach and disinfectant and tins of cat food until he felt the crinkle of cellophane under his fingers. He fumbled for a moment and pulled out two dog chews. The dogs heard him. A plastic dog bed dragged for a second on tiles. Once more Joe held his breath. Paws padded on the wash room floor. When Joe opened the door both dogs were behind it with tails wagging and jaws grinning. He raised a finger to his lips and put a chew in each dog's teeth. Satisfied, they scuttered back to their beds to scoff their surprise treat. The back door key was in the lock, as he'd hoped it would be. Joe turned the key and opened the door a crack. He slipped out.

Once outside Joe leaned against the wall to recover. His heart was beating fast and his breaths were quick. He'd done it. It was a clear night, still and welcoming. He sighed walked on and turned the corner. The stables stood out, blacker in the black darkness. Regan whickered to him when she heard his footsteps. Joe glowered at her and raised his finger to his lips again. He peered over Patch's door. Patch was fast asleep. As Joe unbolted the door Patch quickly raised his head.

"It's okay Patch, it's only me," Joe whispered. Patch staggered to his feet, as most ponies do when they are disturbed from sleep. His eyes were half closed and he swayed for a moment. Joe flung his arms around his warm wide neck. "Oh Patch," was all he managed to moan. Patch didn't speak. He simply put his head on Joe's shoulder and waited for him to explain.

He'd thought something was wrong when Joe had stayed away for three days, but now he'd turned up at the dead of night he was certain of it. Joe let go of Patch's neck and looked him in the eye.

"They want to sell you," he said.

So, that was it. They were going to sell him back to the dreadful Jemima's father and the kid had been too ashamed to come and tell him. Patch hung his head, he'd thought this kid was different. He'd trusted this kid. He'd thought they made a good team. Well, he mused, that's people for you, he should never have trusted one. It served him right. He raised his head.

"Joe," he said, "if they sell me, there's nothing in this for you. You won't get anything out of it, but I don't think I could stand any more of that velvet ribbons stuff. You've been good to me, so just leave my stable door open now and I'll be off."

"No! You don't get it!" Joe insisted, "They don't care ***who*** they sell you to, they just want rid of you."

"So leave the door..!"

"NO!" Joe interrupted, "Just listen! I don't want you to go anywhere! You're the best pony ever! You're my friend! I've crept out to tell you my plan."

Patch stared at Joe, this was all happening very fast.

"What I don't get," Patch confessed, "is ***why*** they want rid of me. I know they'd make some money, but why ***now?*** You're not too big for me yet. I don't eat very much any more. We won the championship. What have I done wrong? I try not to be any trouble." Joe hated hearing his tough, cocky pony sound so upset.

*"* It's not **you, it's me!"**

Patch stared again.

"Well why don't they want to sell you then?" he asked. This was making less and less sense.

"My mum has seen me sneak books out to you and she's heard me talking to you, and she's heard you talk, but she thinks it's me pretending to be you, and then she heard that Jemima thought you could talk, and ..."

"Jemima! I knew it! As soon as I saw that kid at that show I knew she'd get mixed up in."

"Patch!" Joe shouted as loudly as he dared, "Just listen! I'm not supposed to be out here! If they know I'm out here they'll sell you ***tomorrow***. Let me finish!"

The noise had finally woken the big white tomcat, who stretched and pulled himself into a sitting position in the corner. Patch stared again, but Joe had never seen him look so troubled.

"Patch, they think you make children go mad."

"Mad?"

"Nuts, daft, crazy!" Patch's troubled look became a confused one. "How do I make children crazy?"

"You don't!" Joe said and put a hand on Patch's neck. "You don't," he repeated softly, "but unless my mother believes you can talk, she'll keep on believing I'm crazy, and that's why she wants to sell you." Patch stood, trying to take all this in.

"So tell her," Patch answered, it seemed obvious. Joe nodded.

"I already have, but she doesn't believe me. - I know we said no telling," he put in, "but that was then." Patch understood that these were desperate circumstances. "So, will ***you*** tell her?"

This was more than Patch had reckoned on. He was afraid, he'd never been so frightened before, not of lorries or water or dogs, or anything. He didn't trust grown ups. They lied. They were greedy.

"It's the only thing I can think of," Joe urged.

"They might still sell me." Joe nodded. He'd realised this, but it was their only chance. Patch was silent for what seemed like a long time. "Okay," he said at last. Joe flung his arms round Patch and kissed him on the neck.

"Yak! You're as bad as that Jemima!"

"In the morning?" Joe asked. Patch agreed.

Joe felt happier at last, he just had to creep back to bed and his plan would stand a chance. He crept out of the stable and was about to tiptoe across the yard when Patch spoke again.

"Joe! Any other kid that gets up here'll get bucked into orbit!" Joe grinned.

"You called me Joe!" he said. "Twice!"

# CHAPTER THIRTEEN

The following morning his mum walked in.

"How're you feeling love?"

"A bit better" Joe answered truthfully and he smothered a cough so that he'd be allowed to get up.

"What's your tracksuit doing on the floor?"

"I got it out so I could wear it," he said quickly. "I want to get up."

"Okay," she said, "but no going outside."

"I'll get wrapped up," he promised. She gave him one of her don't argue looks and picked his crumpled tracksuit up. He was the only child she knew who could crumple clothes before he wore them.

Joe was on edge all morning. Would Patch speak to his mum even if he wasn't there? She cleared the breakfast things and looked at her watch. "I'll go and muck out," she announced.

"I'll come!" Joe said springing to his feet.

"No you won't," she answered, "I'm not having you in bed for the rest of the week." Joe screwed his face up, but he knew it would make no difference. He threw himself back in his chair.

"Are the horses out?"

"No," his mum answered, "your dad's moving the sheep across the road this morning, so he doesn't want them belting about."

So, Patch would be in when his mum mucked out.

Carol pulled on her waxed jacket and pushed her feet into her wellies. She enjoyed these jobs. She liked her mornings at home. She worked in the bookshop in town Tuesday to Friday afternoons, even during the school holidays, which were nearly over. Robert's farming meant there was always someone to look after Joe. The brash noises and fresh air of the farm were a refreshing contrast to the silent shuffles and holy air of the bookshop.

She opened Patch's stable door and pushed a wheelbarrow into the doorway. She put on his headcollar and tied him to the tie ring. "Sorry Patch, " she said, "I'll be as quick as I can about this." She began forking through the crisp straw. The white tomcat stood up and scratched its right ear, violently shook its head and slunk out.

"That cat's got ear mites," Patch said.

Carol stopped. She looked round. She put the fork down. Her heart was pounding. She felt funny. She walked outside. No one.

"Joe!" she shouted. Nothing. She walked back in. She stared at the pony. No, she was being as daft as Joe was. She picked up the fork and tossed some more straw.

"It's forever scratching its ears," Patch said.

She stopped again. Her stomach felt cold and light. She walked to the door again. There was definitely no one around. She looked at the pony again.

"It needs some drops," it said. This time there was no doubt that the pony had spoken. It looked her in the eye and its mouth moved. Carol leaned against the wall and slid slowly down it until she was sitting in the straw still gazing at the pony. Her throat was tight. She felt sick. "Are you alright?" Patch asked. "You don't look well." Carol managed a nod. She swallowed.

"You do talk," was all she could manage to get out.

"Don't let it worry you, Joe's known for ages," Patch reassured her.

"But that poor Pearce-Jones girl! Everyone thinks she's completely mad."

"Yes," Patch answered, "- its worth bearing in mind ..."

Carol didn't finish the mucking out, she was too shaky. She unclipped Patch's headcollar, moved the wheel barrow and walked into the house. She didn't stop to take off her wellies or her waxed jacket, she shed straw and trod mud though the wash room and kitchen, and slumped in an armchair in the living room. Joe turned to her. Bringing wellies or waxed jackets into the living room was strictly forbidden. She was completely white, except for her lips, which were grey. Patch must have spoken. Joe met his mum's eyes.

"What did he say?" he asked, half dreading the answer. What if Patch had asked to be called sir or sworn at her or something?

"The cat's got ear mites." Joe was silent . Had he heard it right? Ear mites weren't a thing to go into shock about. Ear mites weren't worth trailing muck through the house for. This didn't make sense. Joe shrugged.

"Best get some drops for it then." His mum nodded.

"That's what the pony said," she answered.

Joe made his mum a cup of tea, pulled her wellies off for her and sat on the arm of her chair. Eventually it was his mum who broke the silence. "I'm sorry I thought you were barmy." She gave him a quick hug round the middle. Joe jumped off the chair arm and leapt round the room grunting and making monkey movements.

"I am barmy! See!" His mum managed a weak smile.

"So what do we do about him now?" she asked.

"Well, we can't sell him, can we?"

"I suppose not. It would be like selling a child."

Joe agreed enthusiastically

"And look at the trouble it's caused in our family and the Pearce-Jones family," he added.

"We'll have to convince your dad." Joe nodded again.

They both realised it would be useless to tell him, Patch would have to do it himself.

Joe and his mum went outside together to finish the mucking out. Patch was waiting for them, worried, his ears pricked. When he saw they were both smiling he relaxed a little. They patted him and Joe told him their idea whilst his mum finished off the stable

It was a fairly simple plan. Joe and his mum would go inside as soon as they'd finished their jobs. Joe's dad would arrive at around lunch time to put the horses out after he'd finished with the sheep. This would be Patch's chance to speak. Joe and his mum would be watching from the wash room window. Patch agreed, but he hated all this. It had been bad enough having to speak to ***one*** grown up.

At ten past twelve, Joe's dad strode onto the yard. He was carrying hoof trimmers and dagging shears and Gyp was running at his heels. He put his tools in his pocket, lifted Regan's headcollar from the hook outside her stable and slid it over her nose.

"Come on old girl," he murmured to her. "Time to play out." He wouldn't have spoken at all if he'd known Joe and Carol were spying on him from the wash room. He led Regan out, Taz trotting at her side with the sharp stiletto heeled foal movements that Joe loved. Joe's mum looked at her watch.

"I've to be at work in less than an hour," she giggled.

"Be late," Joe said. "This is important." He was right. His dad reappeared and walked into Patch's stable. He disappeared from view. Joe could feel his heart beating in his throat. All his body felt taut and squeezed in. His mum had fallen quiet too. Then his dad walked out with Patch. Joe looked at his mum in horror. Patch had chickened out! His mum was still staring through the window, her forehead furrowed with anxiety. Then, in a voice as loud and as clear as that of Luciano Pavorotti, Patch spoke. "I can talk you know," he said. He had turned and was looking Robert directly in the face. Robert dropped the leadrope and backed off a pace. Joe's mum made to go to him but Joe put a hand on her arm. He wanted to be certain that his dad was in no doubt.

"I didn't say I bite. I said I talk," Patch added.

Joe's dad backed off another pace - then turned and ran like a whippet, scattering his dagging shears and hoof trimmers as he went!

"Carol! Carol!" he yelled, tripping over the dog, "Carol!", tripping over the washroom doorstep. Carol was in front of him with her hands on his shoulders.

"Calm down, its okay," she was saying. His eyes were the size of frizbees as he glanced back at the pony and at his wife again. He was shaking. He pointed at Patch but no sound came out of his mouth. "It spoke," Carol said for him, and he nodded. "We know, she said, "I'll put the kettle on," and she lead him by his arm to the house, as if he were old or blind.

Joe walked towards Patch - everyone else had forgotten him in the panic - picked up his lead rope and lead him to the gate.

"Thanks," Joe said to him. "That took some guts."

As Joe released him, Patch kicked up his heels and went racing round the field - just like an ordinary pony, Joe thought.

# CHAPTER FOURTEEN

Back in the house, Robert was sitting in the same armchair Carol had been in two hours earlier. He too was wearing his wellies, and greasy overalls. Carol looked round, there was mud and sheep muck trodden into the carpet and she didn't want to think about the state of the armchair.

She explained the whole story to her husband, as far as she could and he had begun to regain some of his colour. Every now and then he shook his head and made along breathy whistle or said something like, "Who'd have thought it." Joe walked in, grinning broadly.

"So, we can't sell him now, can we?" he said, triumphantly throwing himself onto the sofa with a bounce

"Well, not to the Pearce-Joneses anyway," his dad replied. "They won't be able to afford him!" and he rubbed his hands together at the thought of it.

"Robert!" Joe's mum scolded. Robert put down his cup, stood up and took her by the shoulders, just as she had done to him when the pony had sent him scuttering across the yard.

"Carol," he said, "think about it. It's better than winning the lottery. I need only phone a couple of papers and TV stations and they'll be fighting over the story. Think what a film company would pay for a pony like that!"

"You twit," she said pushing his hands from her shoulders. "Look what happened to the Pearce-Jones girl when she said it could talk. They had her to a psychiatrist before she could explain herself. What makes you think it will be any different with you?"

"Because you'll back me up!" he said. They stared at him.

"You're the twits," he shouted. "Think what we could buy! I'd never have to dip another sheep! You'd never have to sell a birthday card again! Joe! Joe! ... You could have that quad you've been wanting, and ... anything else!" He glanced furiously at their blank faces. What was the matter with these two?

"I want that pony," Joe said quietly.

"And I don't mind selling birthday cards," his mum added.

"You can have as many ponies as you want, and you can have your own bookshop! What's the matter with you?"

Joe's mum stared at her husband.

"I'll be late for work," she said, stonily, and she strode off to put on her coat. Joe followed her. "I'll get some drops for the cat while I'm out."

"Don't worry about Patch love, no one will believe him. That pony has more sense than to talk to the press!" She smiled, Joe nodded, she was right but he still felt very uneasy about it all. Why couldn't his dad think more like his mum?

When Joe went back his dad was waiting for him in the living room. Before he could walk past him into the kitchen to make a sandwich, (they'd all missed lunch), his dad placed himself in the kitchen doorway and launched into a speech.

“Listen Joe, one day this place will be yours and I'm telling you, running this farm isn't easy - you know that! I'm up before you most days. At lambing time there are nights when I don't get any sleep. I work Saturdays and Sundays and at haymaking, I can work a fifteen hour day for weeks. I'm back and forth to the auction like a fiddler’s elbow, and it's not even as if the land is any good.

Out in that field is a pony that you'll have out grown in two years. It's not even a good looking pony. If we sell that, you'll never have to break your neck trying to make enough brass out of this moor land to feed a family. We'll be set up. It would have a good life. Anybody paying the sort of money we'll be asking for the pony will look after it. It makes sense Joe." Joe narrowed his eyes.

"Why don't you just sell me instead?"

"Don't be ridiculous Joe, it's illegal to sell children."

Illegal! Was that the only reason he hadn't sold him? Joe pushed past his dad and stomped into the kitchen.

"I'll have a sandwich if you're making one!" his dad shouted after him. Joe pretended he hadn't heard. He could make his own flaming sandwich. Joe slapped tuna fish onto a buttered muffin, wrapped it all in cling film, stuffed it in his pocket and walked out through the wash room. He whistled to the dogs as he went

Yogi knew Joe had something in his pocket and trotted next to him, looking longingly up and occasionally lifting his two front feet off the ground. Joe smacked his nose once or twice, but it made no difference, Yogi didn't give up. Joe took out the sandwich and unwrapped it. A cloud of tuna fish smell hit him. It put him off. He gave it to Yogi who snapped it down in two gulps and looked at Joe for more.

"Pig," Joe said, and then he remembered that was what his dad had said the first time he'd seen Patch.

He wished he could turn back the clock to then. Would it be any different? Well, he'd avoid Great Ulverton show and Jemima Pearce-Jones! Still, it would only have been a matter of time Joe reasoned.

They would have found out somehow, life's like that. Joe looked at Yogi, "I wish my dad could see there are some things more important than money." Yogi put his head on one side. "My mum can see that," Joe went on. Gyp yawned and lay down. Yogi kept staring up at Joe. "She said it would be like selling a child. It would. Mind you, my dad doesn't seem to think there's anything wrong with that. He'd sell me if he could, that's for sure. He'd probably ***farm*** children if it wasn't illegal. A child farm. He'd put them in a trailer and take them to the auction every month. Tight!"

He looked at Gyp. "It's a good job you're a useless sheep dog, or he'd sell you." Gyp wagged his tail. He rambled on at the dogs like this for a while, it made him feel better, then he wandered round the land with the dogs, throwing sticks for them and dabbling in the stream. The afternoon passed slowly and the clouds moved in, Joe had no coat but he didn't want to go back in the house until his mum came home. He brought the horses in at five o'clock and fed them. He was cold. His mum would be furious if she knew he had no coat on.

At quarter to six his mum's battered Fiesta rattled up the lane. Joe wandered into the washroom so she wouldn't know he'd been without a coat all afternoon after he'd just recovered from a cold. She walked in, took off her coat and groped in the pocket for a small bottle which she gave to Joe.

"For the cat," she explained. Joe slipped it in his jeans pocket. "Has he said anything else about Patch?" she asked. Joe shook his head, "I've kept out of his way."

His mum went into the kitchen and made sausage and chips for herself and Joe.

Whilst they were eating them at the kitchen table his dad walked in and looked around. He walked over to the grill and looked in, then he did the same with the microwave.

"Where's mine?" he asked finally. Joe's mum looked up.

"You know where the fridge is."

"Is this all because of that blasted pony?" he demanded. Joe kept his eyes fixed on his plate.

"This," Carol answered, "is because I don't much feel like doing ***anything*** for you at the moment. You have no idea how to value things, have you? You don't even value me. I work all day and then come home and feed you, and to you that's nothing is it?" Robert looked amazed.

***"I*** don't know the value of things**?** ***I don't ?*** I'm trying to tell ***you*** the value of that pony."

"No you're not!" Carol snapped. "You're trying to tell me how much money it will fetch! - And the sad thing is you don't even know the difference."

"The sad thing is," he bellowed, "I've got no dinner!"

She and Joe carried on eating in silence. Robert went to the fridge took out an egg and fried it. Carol stood, picked up her plate and Joe's, put them in the sink, picked up the frying pan and threw Robert's egg in the bin. Robert moved his mouth like a goldfish would but no sound came out. He went to the fridge, took out another egg and fried it. Carol picked up the pan and threw the egg in the bin. Robert picked up his car keys.

"I'm going for some chips!" he shouted, furious.

"What're you worried about?" Carol yelled back. "Eggs are only worth about ten pence each!"

Joe hated it when his mum and dad argued. He knew his mum was right but he didn't want her to treat his dad like this.

Robert ate his chips in the car to stop Carol getting her hands on them. Carol moved the lace curtain and chuckled to herself at the sight of him eating chips from a newspaper in the Land Rover.

# CHAPTER FIFTEEN.

Carol made him no breakfast the next morning and Robert made his own as noisily as he could - after he'd found the Shredded Wheat, which took him ten minutes. Carol couldn't disguise her humour. As she sat at the breakfast table her shoulders shook with the furious and futile slamming of every cupboard. If his dad had ***asked*** where the Shredded Wheat were, Joe would have told him, but he didn't ask. When he'd finished slopping milk about he walked to the telephone.

"London. BBC and ITV headquarters, please." Joe shot a horrified glance at his mum. She smiled.

"Don't worry," she said, "he'll never get away with it." A few seconds later they heard his dad speaking again,

"I'd like to speak to someone in connection with the ***Country file*** programme ... yes, it concerns an item which they may be interested in reporting ... yes, I'll hold."

Joe and his mum had crept into the living room and were now standing just inside the door, out of sight but within good hearing range.

"Yes, my name's Robert Cooper, I farm eighty two acres in the West Pennines and I have an item you may be interested in covering. Certainly, it's a talking pony

.... a talking pony ... that's right .. No, no, it actually talks with its mouth, like you and me ... Hello? hello?... are you there?" - He slammed the receiver down.

Joe's mum gave them away by bursting into laughter.

"Told you so!" she grinned at her husband, but as he wasn't speaking to her there was nothing he could do but give her a cold hard stare. Still staring at her, he very deliberately picked up the receiver again and, looking at the numbers he'd written on a pad by the phone, he dialled again.

Joe and his mum were now sitting on the bottom step of the stairs grinning openly at him as he addressed the person at the other end. "Hello, can I speak to someone in connection with ***The Really Wild Show*** please? Hello, I have an item which you may want to cover, its a talking pony .. No, no it actually talks, with its lips ... What do you mean? ***"What does it say",*** it depends what you've asked it! (Joe and his mum began to giggle) It's not like a parrot!, I've not ***taught*** it to talk, it just ***does*** ... Yes, that's right, it can hold a conversation ... (There was a long pause) Because we haven't put a flaming phone extension in its stable, that's why!"

By now Joe had rolled off the bottom step and was lying on his side holding his stomach with the agony of stifling his laughter. His mum was lying on her back laughing aloud and stamping on the floor. Joe's dad glared at them both and banged down the receiver. His mum managed to drag herself into a sitting position and wipe the tears from her eyes, she looked up at her husband.

"Look," she said, "admit when you're beaten."

"Who's beaten?" he said.

"Oh well," Carol grinned, "I can't spend all morning out here laughing at you, much as I'd love to, there's a house to be cleaned and stables to be mucked out," and she walked off, still chuckling to herself.

Joe put the TV on. It was children's holiday programmes and if he left the sound low, he could still hear the conversation in the hall. There wasn't much to hear in fact. Every three minutes or so his father slammed the receiver down in a huff. Eventually though, one conversation caught his attention.

"Yes, yes I'd be delighted ... this afternoon would be fine." Joe's dad couldn't resist walking into the living room doorway and winking at Joe, giving him the thumbs up and tapping the side of his nose with his forefinger as he gave directions to the farm. This time it was his dad's turn to grin. Joe jumped up and ran out to tell his mum. His dad called after him.

"Tell your mum to leave that pony in! There's a reporter coming this afternoon!"

"Tell her yourself," Joe bawled in the safe knowledge that he was out of walloping distance.

Out in the stables his mum was completely unconcerned.

"So what?" she said. "Joe, we had that pony for five months before I got a peep out of it, so what do you think a reporter will get out of it in five minutes?"

"Well, put him out anyway," Joe urged.

"No, we'll leave him in like your dad said, there's no point in getting him more annoyed than he already is." Joe walked over to Patch,

"Patch, don't say a word to the man who comes in this afternoon, promise." Patch answered with his mouth full of hay.

"As if I would," he said.

Joe followed his mum back into the house. His dad was in the - now dirty - armchair, nursing a cup of coffee and grinning from ear to ear.

"Have you left it in?" he asked.

Carol nodded and picked up what she assumed was her coffee.

"Sunday Scandal - they believed me!"

Carol coughed and spat her coffee all over the arm of the dirty armchair.

"The Sunday Scandal believed that Martians had landed in Wolverhampton and the Queen Mother is secretly married to Cliff Richard!" she screeched.

"So?" his dad said, looking injured at being laughed at yet again.

"So, what are they paying you?"

"Well, they have to *see* it first of course."

"Of course," Carol agreed, "of course."

# CHAPTER SIXTEEN

Joe's mum had gone to work when, at two o'clock, a large blue Volvo drew into the yard and a man of about forty got out armed with a mini tape recorder. He was wearing a threadbare blue jacket and a V-necked pullover. For all the world like a teacher, Joe thought.

Robert scurried out to meet him. He was wearing his checked sports jacket and a flat cap, the gentleman farmer look, he called it. They shook hands and walked, talking, shoulder to shoulder, round the corner to the stable yard. Joe could hear snippets:

"Likes to have ***Horse and Hound*** read to him ... only heard it myself in the last few days ... my son mostly."

Joe glowered, If they asked him he'd deny it all, say his dad was potty. He noticed his dad had quickened his pace when they passed him. They disappeared inside Patch's stable. Joe stood outside, he could see what was going on but he wasn't quite close enough to hear, which was a pity because if he had, he'd have had another good laugh.

"So, this is the chap is it?" the reporter asked. "Get him to say something will you?" and he flicked his mini tape recorder on and held it at Patch's nose.

Patch leaned forward and bit it.

"Oi! Can't you control it!" the reporter yelled.

"Sorry," Joe's dad apologised and he tapped Patch on the nose. "Don't do that," he said, as you would to any pony. The reporter checked and shook his machine.

"No damage. So, go on then, get it to talk."

Patch munched his hay. Robert patted the pony's neck. He suddenly felt foolish. What had made him think he could get this pony to talk? He grinned at the reporter, it was somewhere between an apology and a weak attempt at being friendly.

"I don't think he's in the mood," Robert said. The reporter glared at him, "Well, he's got ten minutes to get in the mood, because I'm covering a divorcee who poured wet concrete in her ex-husbands underpants at three thirty, and I've got to get to Leeds for that."

"It does talk," Robert insisted, "but it talks to my son really. Joe!" As soon as Joe heard his name, he bolted for the wash room door. By the time, his dad had reached the stable door and called again, Joe had gone.

Joe looked down from his bedroom window. He saw the reporter walking determinedly towards his Volvo, his dad half walking half running behind him. Every now and then, he swung round and called Joe's name. The car drove off, probably to Leeds and the concrete underpants.

Joe's dad stomped towards the front door. Quickly Joe dashed downstairs, slipped out the back and turned Patch out. He kept out of his dads way for the afternoon, he was getting good at that. Joe's mum came home late and laden with shopping bags. Joe dashed to her car.

"You were right!" he said. "They didn't believe him." She grinned, "Told you!" she said with a wink.

When they went indoors, his dad was sulking. Carol pretended innocence.

"How did it go?" she enquired,

"As if you care!"

"I do care!" she said, "I want to keep that pony,"

"Well, it looks like you will and you'll keep your battered car and your lousy job as well because no one believes me."

"Get away. You don't say," she answered with as much sarcasm as she could muster.

"I'm fed up with this!" Robert bellowed, "I'm going to fetch the horses in!"

Joe went to follow him. He'd rather bring Patch in himself. "Leave him," Joe's mum advised. "He's better off on his own." As Robert had grudgingly agreed they'd be keeping the pony, Carol decided she'd give him a meal this evening. She'd bought salmon quiche and salad.

Joe finished unpacking the shopping and Carol prepared the salad. There was no sign of Robert, so she covered his plate with cling film. She and Joe finished eating and Joe loaded the dishwasher. His mum glanced through the kitchen window, Robert was taking his time. Probably still sulking. She and Joe went to sit in the living room. She'd just unfolded the Evening News when she heard the click of the wash room door. Carol stood up in order to tell Robert where to find his dinner, but Robert wasn't there. Yogi and Gyp had come back alone. Carol fussed them. He must be in a really foul mood if the dogs couldn't stand his company.

"Shall I go and look for him and tell him his dinner's ready?"

"No," Carol said, "it's not as if it's going cold. He's better left alone when he's like this. Even the dogs have worked that out."

"But the dogs don't usually come home on their own do they mum?" "They do if he's kicked them! You've watched too many Lassie films." Joe laughed, she was right, it's not as if they were whining and pawing at his legs!

They watched the regional news and *Coronation Street*. Every creak and click made Joe turn to the door to greet his dad - but he was never there. As the advertisements came on his mum went into the kitchen to make herself a cup of tea. Joe looked up and saw that the blue of the sky was deepening. He followed his mum into the kitchen and glanced through the window, the cars were both there, he hadn't gone out, but the horses still weren't in their stables. His mum wasn't alarmed. "Take no notice, he could sulk for England Joe," was all she said. Just as she did so there was a clatter of hooves, it was Patch. Joe ran out to the yard.

"You'd better come!" Patch said, he sounded breathless, "Your dad is lying in the field." His mum had followed Joe out.

"I'll phone an ambulance," she called. As Joe turned to run Patch stopped him.

"Jump up," he said. Joe vaulted up and grasped Patch's mane.

Patch galloped over the fields to where Joe's dad lay face down in the mud, his body wedging open the gate. Joe slipped down and bent over his father's body.

His dad was still breathing, but he was very cold.

Joe tried to remember what he'd learnt in school. His mind raced through the instructions in the leaflet he'd been given. ***"Casualty unconscious but breathing, place in recovery position and keep warm"***

Joe pushed his father's heavy limbs into the recovery position and took off his sweatshirt to tuck round him. At the same time, his mum arrived carrying a duvet. His mum covered his dad up and Joe turned to Patch. "How long has he been ***here?"***

"I don't know," Patch said. (He looked worried, even though Robert was no friend of his.) "I thought it was getting late so I came up to the gate to see where everybody was."

"Look." Joe's mum pointed to Regan who was grazing a few yards away. A leadrope was trailing from her headcollar. Joe was beginning to build up a picture of what had happened. His dad had gone to get Regan and as he was leading her out of the field, he'd fallen, or she'd been startled and pushed him and he'd hit his head, probably on the gate post. Knowing this didn't make him feel any better.

In the distance, his mum spotted the blue light of an ambulance. She started back towards the farmhouse to meet the paramedics.

# CHAPTER SEVENTEEN

Joe sat on the floor next to his grandma. She was the only person in the world who was allowed to stroke his hair.

She'd been sent for so that his mum could go to the hospital.

It was half past ten. Joe should have been in bed more than an hour ago but his grandma had said that there was no point, she'd said he wouldn't be able to sleep anyway. She was right. Each slight sound sent Joe's head swivelling to look at the door. A telephone rang on television and Joe jumped up. There was a film on, but neither of them was watching it.

His grandma spoke.

"So, tell me again, how could you tell that your pony wanted you to follow it?"

"Well, it neighed and looked worried. It as good as ***told*** us."

"Well who'd have believed it? And your dad wants to sell it - eh? All because he thinks its worth a bob or two. He always was a grabbing little beggar. He was the same when he was a lad. He's always been one for making a fast quid.

He used to go on the golf club after it had shut, and collect stray golf balls. He'd sell them back to the golfers of a Sunday morning. The daft ha'porths were buying their own golf balls back!"

Joe laughed.

"Still, he's done all right for himself, your dad, hasn't he? This lovely farm, and you!"

Joe crawled onto the sofa and squashed himself between the chair arm and his grandma.

"You're a big softy," she said. ***"You'll*** never make any money," and she gave him a squeeze.

"I'm not bothered," Joe answered. "Money isn't everything. If my dad had sold Patch, he might be dead now. He'd have sold me if it wasn't illegal." His grandma laughed.

"It's not a joke, it's true. He said so."

"You must have got it wrong. He wouldn't do that."

Joe was quiet for a while. "Do you think he'll be all right?"

"Course he will!" his grandma said, hugging him. "He might be tight fisted but he's as tough as old boots!"

Yogi heaved himself onto the sofa. He'd become too hot by the fire. Yogi and Gyp loved it when grandma baby-sat. It was the only time they were allowed into the living room. "Poor little beggars," she'd say, "come and have a warm."

It was ten past twelve when the front door opened. Joe had nodded off on his grandma's shoulder. He sat up swiftly.

"What are those damned dogs doing in here?" his mum asked as she unbuttoned her coat.

"How is he Carol?"

"He's come round."

Joe jumped up flung his arms round his mum and burst into tears. "Hey, you were supposed to cry when he was at death's door! Not now.

Now, get those dogs shifted, they'll think its Christmas."

His grandma kissed Joe on the cheek.

"Night night, sleep tight, hope the bugs don't bite," she said.

She called the dogs to the wash room whilst Joe stumbled sleepily up the stairs.

"He'll be home in a day or two, they just want to keep an eye on him for a bit," his mum explained.

The next morning when Joe awoke he lay staring at the ceiling. He was glad his dad was okay but he felt all mixed up. Why had he cried when his mum came home? He'd felt relieved but he'd still cried. He couldn't stop thinking about the pony.

When he'd found his dad in the field he'd thought he was dead, and he'd not even ***worried*** about Patch then.

If he'd been dead, would it have been his fault? His dad had gone out in a temper because he was mad about Patch. Was that Joe's fault? Was it Patch's fault? It depended how far you thought back.

Joe sat up, swung his feet out of bed and stood up. He grabbed his dressing gown and padded barefoot downstairs. When he got into the living room, he stopped. He could hear his mum. "My fault you know. If he'd not gone out in such a temper it probably wouldn't have happened. I thought he was just sulking. All night Joe kept telling me to go and look for him, but I didn't take any notice. He could have been ***dead."***

He couldn't let his mum think like that.

"It wasn't your fault mum," he said as he walked in.

"It wasn't anybody's fault," his grandma said firmly. "I had many a row with your granddad in our time, but I never knocked myself unconscious after one. It doesn't follow."

Joe smiled at his grandma's brutal common sense.

"There's neither of you should be blaming yourselves. And I'll tell you summat else - that pony is a little ***star.*** I'll tell your dad that an' all. It should be on the television!"

Joe and his mum burst out laughing.

Grandma started to throw rashers of bacon in a pan and to mutter about lads of Joe's age needing a cooked breakfast down them.

Joe's mum walked to the door, she was off to do the morning round of the farm.

“What wants doing while you're out Carol, besides the washing up?" grandma asked.

“Nothing," Carol answered as she pulled on her wellies. "We've a machine to do the washing up. Leave it."

"I'll give that armchair a scrub then. It’s a disgrace," grandma said with a smile. "And that living room carpet could do with a shampooing."

Carol stopped. "Do you know, I was bothered about that mucky armchair until yesterday, but when somebody you love comes *that* close - well, you realise what’s important, don't you? - and armchairs aren't." Grandma stopped pushing the bacon round the pan for a few seconds and murmured in agreement. Carol put on her coat and walked out. The wash room door banged closed.

"I hope I've not spoken out of turn. I'll give it a scrub anyway," grandma said, as the greasy bacon slithered onto Joe's plate. "I don't like to sit idle."

In the promised two days Joe's dad returned home, hardly the worse for wear. Joe's mum insisted that he should rest in bed for a few more days, that she and Joe could manage the farm and that the doctor said he wasn't ready for work yet.

Robert hated that. If he'd *chosen* to, he'd sit with his nose in a newspaper for hours, but newspapers lost all their interest when there was nothing to do *but* read them. So Joe kept his dad company whenever he could.

He took a gruesome interest in the bruise on his dad's temple. It was purple in the middle with a circle of blue around that, and the outside edge, just where it met the hair in one place, was yellow. He prodded it.

"Does that hurt?"

"Yes it does!" his dad snapped, snatching his head away. Then he moaned and held his head in his hands because such sudden movement made it ache.

"What's a blood clot dad?"

"Like a lump of blood."

"Is it sticky?"

"I suppose so."

"Ugh! Is it like a scab?"

"How do I know?"

"How can you tell if you've got a blood clot?"

"You die."

"So why did they think you might have a blood clot? You're not dead."

"I don't know! I didn't get one did I - Can we change the subject please?" Joe didn't know what else to talk about. He'd deliberately not mentioned Patch so far, because he was afraid it might annoy his dad, but he'd annoyed him now anyway, by talking about blood clots.

"The ambulance man said that if we'd not found you when we did you could have died."

"I know," his dad said, "and you and your mum were gawping at *Coronation Street*! It's a good job that pony's not as daft as you two."

"It has its uses after all, doesn't it?" Joe said.

His dad smiled.

"So, no more phone calls?" he wheedled, narrowing his eyes.

“I'd already decided that," his dad agreed. "When I was in hospital, one thing kept going through my mind."

"What?"

"What your mum said about knowing what's important. It’s a pity it's taken me till I'm forty to work it out. Patch can stay here as long as he wants, so long as he makes you happy."

"I'll go out and tell him."

Joe thundered downstairs and jumped the last three steps. He landed in a crouch, bounced up and zigzagged past the furniture in the living room, his mother in the kitchen, and the dogs in the wash room. He walloped the wash room door back with such force it smashed against the wall. By the time he heard the noise it made he was already half way across the yard.

He stood at the field gate, cupped his hands round his mouth and bawled, "Pa . .aaa.... tch!" Patch raised his head.

"Come here!"

Patch began to amble across the field. Joe clambered over the gate. "Quick!" Patch picked up a slow trot and arrived next to Joe with an amused look on his face.

“What’s so important?" he asked.

“You can stay!" Joe shouted, hugging him. There was a pause before Patch answered.

"And what am I supposed to do in return? Talk to newspaper reporters? Appear on TV?"

"No! Nothing! Just let me ride you!"

“Same as before?"

"Same as before!"

"Does your dad know?"

"It was my dad's ***idea."***

"What's in it for him then?"

"Patch if it wasn't for you he'd be dead. He knows that. That bash on his head has done him good."

"And when you are too big to ride me?"

"You can stay ***here!"*** Patch nodded in quiet agreement and went back to grazing.

The white tomcat leapt onto the fence next to Joe.

"Did you hear that, Cat?" Joe said, stroking its back, "Your friend can stay"

"Good," the cat said, "I've enjoyed having someone to talk to."